THE FIVE FINGER
MOUNTAINS

COMING IN **2022** AND **2023**...

The Five Finger Mountains:
The Story of Haven
Book II

The Five Finger Mountains:
The Night of the Hunters
Book III

For more information go to:

www.fivefingermountains.com

THE FIVE FINGER MOUNTAINS

BOOK I

BY
TYKE

ISBN Paperback: 978-1-7377817-0-7
ISBN Hardcover: 978-1-7377817-1-4
ISBN eBook: 978-1-7377817-2-1

Edited By: Nicole Kimble Wilson
Book Cover and Interior Design: Creative Publishing Book Design
Cover Art and Illustrations: Bogdan Maksimovic

Printed in the United States of America

In memory of…

Sookie, Buzzie, and Frank
And to I AM… who is the light in the darkness

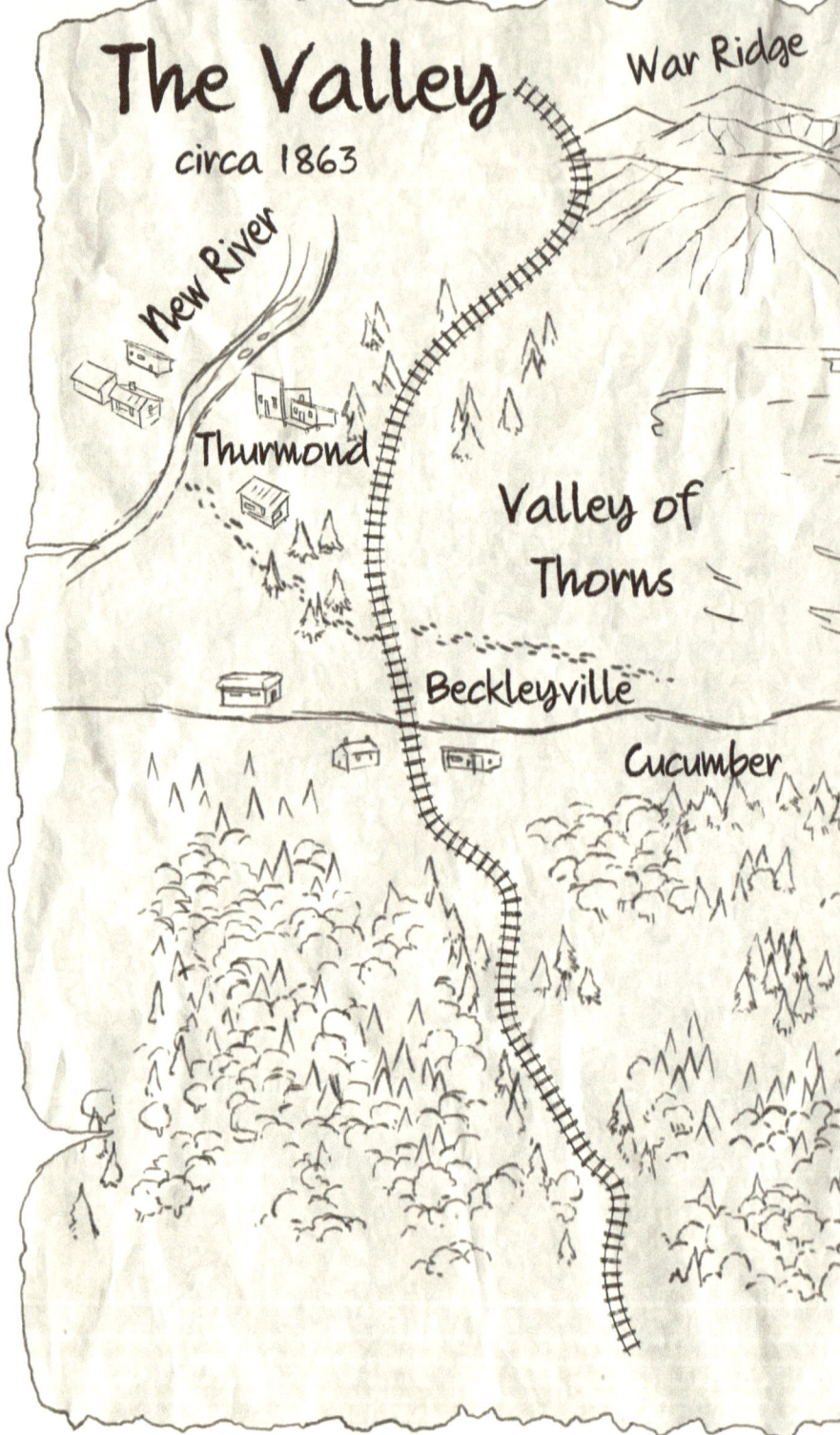

Droop Mountain
Five Fingers Mountain
Greenbrier River
Sam Black Church
Old Beckley Road
Lewisburg

Prologue

It was midnight with a blood red moon. The boy on top of the mountain ran downhill as fast as he could. His skin was gone from both his knees and shins, and the blood that had once soaked through his clothes had dried long ago. He knew that if he fell, he was too weak to ever get back up.

The boy's uniform was soaked in sweat. His jacket was in shreds from the dozens of tiny claws that had ripped away the fabric, exposing his torn flesh. As the boy ran, he sobbed uncontrollably. He was scared – more frightened than he had ever been in his life. All the death and destruction he had seen recently filled him with terror. Afraid of the kiss of death.

He heard a twig snap, and stopped short, jerking his head to the right. The sound startled him. He did not think they were that close. For a moment, he imagined he saw those eyes. But nothing came at him.

At least not yet.

He stopped and turned to face the trail, catching his breath, and then started running again. He couldn't stop long. He knew they were very, very close.

As he stumbled wildly in the darkness, he thought he saw a small light up ahead. The light went out for a moment, only to reappear once again. If he could get to the light, perhaps he could rest. Maybe even look for a small creek or water hole to get a drink. He was so thirsty. It seemed like years since he had something to drink.

Once again, the boy heard a twig snap. This time it was behind him and to the left. "Shit" he hissed under his breath. He quickened his pace, now running at a sprint.

If only he could make it to the light. If only he could run a little faster. "God, please let me make it. PLEASE!" he begged into the darkness as he ran. What seemed like an hour (but in fact was only minutes) he collapsed into a clearing where a small campfire burned. The last thing he saw before passing out was her face.

◇

My name is Reece and this is my story.
For he…was me.

CHAPTER 1
My Beginning

That almost seems like it happened to another person, in another universe, years gone by on the backside of time. Back then, it was the spell of war, so palatable that it reeked.

Now as you read on, let my story serve as more of a warning. We must remember times past so we can teach the unborn our mistakes.

Back and forth they went. Yankee and Reb. It took me a lifetime, but I had to learn the final lesson…that ultimately, we are all Americans. We all fight similar battles. It makes no difference the color of our skin, the background of our fight, the utter indifference of mankind.

There is far, far worse.

I witnessed children with sharp-pointed rifles. Solders dressed in blue and grey bringing death and destruction. Mankind's sacred bearing bondage and suffering. Slavery dressed in an immoral, evil coat of white satin.

But this story, well *my* story, flows much deeper. For it was filled with vengeance, and the treachery runs deeper than you would ever imagine. My story did not end, nor begin, then. We must go back to understand what lay ahead…and what lies in wait, still, for us all.

◦◌

My name is Reece, and age has caught up with me. In 1863 I was a young, naïve 14-year-old boy. But now I feel antiquated. Ancient. And alone. I live in solace, tucked away from most of mankind. Keeping to myself.

Watching and waiting… for his legions…and him.

I was born on November 5, 1849, in a small Quaker town in Pennsylvania known as Gravity. Pa became acknowledged by God the day of my birth and was ordained a minister the following year. My mother ran a small seamstress store. In 1852 she died of rheumatic fever. I really never knew her.

However, after my mother's death, my Pa, who was refined, lost the revelation. His "inner light" was extinguished. Thereafter, he worshiped in silence. The "Christ within" was replaced with the "Christ without" – and the whiskey. Yielded by the drink, he would sit alone by the fire softly talking to himself, pleading for my Ma. So terrible a sight that through the years I (and later on, Boone and Caleb) would often have to lead him to bed, broken and all alone. But Pa was very honorable, and was smart as hell when it came to teaching both words and numbers.

I…well…I was not. As a boy of 14, my interest laid elsewhere.

Having lost much of his faith, Pa packed me up and we left town, not ever to return. In the earlier years, like gypsy moths, we wandered from flame to flame. However, we eventually settled in a place called Cucumber, Virginia. A "worn-out boot" kind of town with little to no expectations. Passing through, we noticed that the locals were searching for a headmaster for a true, old-fashioned, one-room schoolhouse. My father qualified, and accepted the position.

As I grew older my father became the one true guiding light in a life filled with no one else. "When you teach your son" he would say "You teach your son's son." My father's steady love and wisdom imprinted on my heart and mind, and no matter what happened, I always found myself returning to his words.

Mountains surrounded all sides of Cucumber. The northern range was known as *War Ridge*, named after an Indian battle. To the east, the countryside became much more level, with intermittent cabins and farms scattered throughout. Further east was the town of Lewisburg and past that, Richmond. Nearly all of the wealthy lived in Richmond. Pa always said that there was lots of "old money" in Richmond.

The south was mining country, with farms and cabins carved into hillsides where people would search for the black coal found deep in the ground. This seemed to occupy most of their time. Because of the rough terrain, and due to the fact that there were few byways, I did not travel much to this area. Around 15 miles west lay Beckleyville, a somewhat larger town than Lewisburg. Beckleyville was slightly more difficult to travel to because there was only one road, which was often washed out due to rain or heavy snow.

And to the north east of *War Ridge* were the Five Finger Mountains. A profane blemish overlooking a desolate basin called the Valley of Thorns. The mountains were uninhabited, isolated, and covered in fog most days. No one ever, *ever*, traveled to the Five Finger Mountains. Not to hunt, not to fish, and not to build. "There is evil there that does not sleep. You young ins stay out of there." Mounds – who owned the only boarding house – would say. "There's no need to go up to that Godforsaken place." Caleb bequeathed her the nickname because of her "shoulder boulders" (his words, not mine).

As boys, we listened to the warnings about the Five Finger Mountains, but the words didn't settle anywhere in our minds – they went in one ear and out the other, like a breeze through the leaves.

Still now, so many years later, I find myself longing for the naivety and ignorance of those youthful days, before the word turned upside down.

∾

Back then, the town of Cucumber consisted of a post office, several general stores, the school, and Kate's boarding house, i.e., "the Mounds house." We lived just outside of town, on Little Dog Lane. We boasted a front wooden picket fence, two large chestnut trees, and a full front-covered porch.

Pa and I were very happy during our time in Cucumber.

I had two best friends, both of whom I met when we first moved to town. Well, actually I had three best friends until my dog, Lilly succumbed to a snake bite. The other two friends were brothers, and were as different as chocolate is to vanilla. The older one by six years was Boone. He was a behemoth.

At 16 years old, he was well over six feet tall and weighed over 275 pounds. He dwarfed most men and certainly any boy of that age. I once saw him bust up a chifforobe in less than one minute.

Boone was also as gentle as a giant.

Caleb was Boone's younger brother. Where Boone was, well, *huge*, Caleb was of normal height and weight of any boy of 10. He was extremely shy and reserved, and when excited, he would stutter. In class the children would cruelly call him a "Stuttering Stanley." Caleb (mostly) was a boy of few words.

The two had no immediate family, so they became my brothers. They stayed some of the time at Mounds but, more often than not, they stayed with Pa and me. Boone and Caleb were the ones who taught me how to hunt, fish, and play the knife game "Mumblety-Peg." Players start from the end finger and flip the knife over until the blade sticks firmly in the ground. The player moves on and follows the progression to the next finger, then the next finger, then the wrist, elbow, shoulder, and nose. If the player gets this far in the game, they start from the nose and go down the other side of the body. Naturally, if you miss, you have to start all over again. Both Boone and Caleb were masters of the Mumblety-Peg.

We constantly played this game and as brothers do, they taught me to always carry my knife.

It was this habit that ultimately helped keep me alive.

CHAPTER 2
Sarah

By the time I was fourteen I began to realize that there was more to the world than hunting, fishing, and eating. And in my world, her name was Sarah. She was the prettiest girl in all of Virginia. In school we had only two teachers, aside from my father. Sarah would sit up front, always in the same seat, while I usually sat in the rear with Boone and Caleb. Occasionally, she would throw us a glance, bat her eyes, and giggle at our absurdities. Boone and I would often debate which boy she would prefer. Bewildered by the whole spectacle, Caleb would make a face and act like he was going to gag.

As Southerners, we listened to the talk of the Rebellion, or as a very true Southerner would say, the "War of Northern Aggression." It was the year 1863, and the most horrific and bloodiest year of this civil war had yet to begin. In January, President Abraham Lincoln enacted the Emancipation Proclamation, and the South answered in May with the Union defeat in Chancellorsville.

At the time, we thought that we Southerners were invincible.

In class, Pa said that this was a struggle between two opposing interests within a single nation. He explained that it had developed into two distinct issues: the question of slavery and the question of state's rights.

However, I now know there was a third issue, far more sinister than that. A problem in which I call the *Great Disconnect.* A problem which was very apparent to those living in the small mountain communities. It was a matter of opportunity – and wealth. Those located in the more built up, well-to-do towns and settlements of the South felt that they were of a higher breed, of better stock. That they were superior to us.

Most Southerners in Western Virginia believed that slavery was an abomination of God's Law. Hell, most hadn't even ever *seen* a slave. There were many, Pa and I included, that wanted to distance themselves from that small, privileged, and oppressive ruling class of Virginia.

However, for our beliefs, the town of Cucumber had to pay a price.

⚶

On October 30, 1863, I awoke with a bright morning sun kissing the windows. I remember the date so well because there was to be an All-Hallows E'en dance at Old Man Clover's barn that night, and to get an early start on the preparations Pa had already left for school. Humming an old song Pa sang to me as a baby, I ate a quick breakfast, fixed my lunch pail with roasted trout, and started off for school.

As I walked, I dreamed of Sarah and imagined us dancing the night away. In my imagination, we would sneak off behind the barn, where she would let me steal a kiss. Those bright blue eyes, full lips, and long blonde hair drove me crazy.

I was so lost in my thoughts that it took me a while to notice the ground was covered in locusts. With large, bulbous eyes, incandescent wings, and long thick bodies, they offered a heightened degree of curiosity for a young boy. I wondered if they would make good fishing bait, so I stuffed four in my overall pockets and, realizing that I was going to be late for class, ran the rest of the way to school.

Although slightly late, my arrival did not cause much of a stir because everyone was talking about the up-and-coming dance. I remember that it was really hard for me to sit still that day. I kept looking over to Sarah – she avoided looking back. I repeatedly asked Boone and Caleb if it was lunch, but they kept telling me to hush up. I felt that the minutes were turning into days.

Two hours into class, our teacher, Ms. MacCulcah (she taught Math and English) was going over the definition of a proper-noun. It was then I felt something wiggling out of my pocket. I looked down just in time to see the first of the four locusts trying to escape the prison of my pocket, where they had been held captive since morning. I quickly grabbed the first bug and examined it. It appeared to blink at me with its large eyes. Suddenly it dawned on me that I could get Sarah's attention and find out if she was going to the dance by throwing the two-winged creature at her desk. While Ms. MacCulcah had her back to the class, I launched the flying devil towards the front of the class.

It didn't go quite as planned.

The locust overshot Sarah and landed square in the middle of Ms. MacCulcah's back. Luckily, she was wearing a long-sleeved sweater. Unbelievable as it sounds, at the time, I really wasn't worried about her. I was upset that I failed at getting Sarah's attention. "Damn," I muttered under my breath, looking around. So far, no one was looking. I took a second locust from my pocket. I drew back and fired the missile, missing again! This time the creature landed just above Ms. MacCulcah's rear end, on her lower back. I looked over at Caleb and Boone. They were busy drawing in their notebooks. Sarah had her head down and also seemed to be writing what was on the chalkboard.

Again, no one noticed.

With good fortune still on my side, I took the third bug in my hand, and with as much focus as I could muster, flung the creature toward Sarah. Again, I missed, and the locust landed on Ms. MacCulcah's right shoulder. It was then that I noticed the other two locusts were traveling up her sweater toward the back of her neck. I reached to get the fourth locust from my pocket, but as I looked up, all eyes but Ms. MacCulcah's were on me.

In times of great trouble, some people panic. But I must say, I remained calm. I looked around the room and, aside from some hushed giggling, silence prevailed.

In every class there are a small few who strive to be the teacher's pet. Those brown-nose offspring who believe that they will become massively successful in life if they rat out those of us who do not uphold their levels of moral excellence. Several of these "pets" immediately raised their hands to inform Ms. MacCulcah of her impending doom. However, she was too busy with the lecture and assignment of the day to notice. Ms. MacCulcah, who was right-handed, had yet to notice the bulbous bugs crawling up her shoulder.

The informants of the class starting making noise. Small, low-keyed coughs started popping up, and as she turned to face the class, all hell broke loose.

As soon Ms. MacCulcah faced us, one of the demon bugs crawled around her right shoulder, peering at her with those big bug eyes. She let out such a scream that I am sure folks in Richmond could hear. She began to slap at the locust on her shoulder when the second bug leaped-frogged over the first one and landed in her hair. She let out another scream and began dancing around the front of the room, knocking over books and papers on her desk and a big globe located in the corner of the room.

I now know where the rebel yell came from.

Ms. MacCulcah kept on swinging and swatting at everything on and around her, frantically moaning, screaming, and snorting all at once. No one could understand anything she was saying. It was then that she grabbed her hair to try and get any bugs out of it when her entire head of hair fell off – a wig! Looking at the class and realizing that she had no hair was too much for Ms. MacCulcah. She let out a final bloodcurdling scream and ran out of the room.

I sat there, stupefied. Pure silence enveloped the room. It seemed that all eyes were on me. As I glanced around, I saw that there were mixed facial expressions, ranging from horror (mostly from the girls in the class) to amusement (and mostly from the boys). Boone, who sat on my right, muttered something like, "You're unbelievable," but I was so stunned that it seemed that everything moved in slow motion.

It was about this time that my father came in to the room.

CHAPTER 3

Ah, Hell

Having been in my fair share of trouble, I knew that Pa would look for me the minute he entered the room. So, I looked over at my friend, Theodore "Jed" Williams, and raised both my hands up, giving Pa the impression that Jed threw the locusts. He took the bait. Pa looked at Jed and loudly exclaimed, "YOU!" He seemed somewhat unsure, and he looked at Boone and yelled, "And YOU!" Finally, with his eyes narrowing and his mouth frowning, he stared directly at me and hissed, "And YOU! Come with me to my office – NOW."

We shuffled to Pa's office, heads down, staring at the floor. If I could just get Boone's attention, we could pin this all on Jed. I gently bumped into Boone and keeping my voice low, muttered, "We can get out of this. Just keep a level head, and follow my lead."

He kept his head down and mumbled something to the effect that I am a horse's ass.

14

Pa ushered Jed into his office first. He glanced at me, and with a stern voice, said, "You boys wait here while I tend to Mr. Williams." Jed frowned at us, and Boone and I could see the dread etched across his face. We both knew that he was toast.

As the door closed, I turned to Boone and said, "We can claim that the windows were left open somehow and that a swarm of locusts blew in, with several landing on Ms. MacCulcah."

"Is that your best explanation?" he asked incredulously. "That's it? That's all you got?"

I nodded and shrugged.

"We are so in the soup," he whined, putting his head in his hands.

A few moments later, the door swung open and Jed walked out with a slight, sly smile on his face. I just knew that that rotten, flea-bitten son of a gun turned me in.

'BOONE!' yelled Pa from inside his office. "YOU'RE NEXT!"

Jed left to head back to class, and Boone turned to me and whispered, "That's the lamest excuse I've ever heard. I ain't going to confess, neither." With his head held high, Boone walked into Pa's office and closed the door behind him.

I had to think quick. Suddenly, I heard an angelic voice say, "Can't blame it on anyone other than YOU, Mr. Reece Ragland!" I turned, and there facing me with a slight smile on her face, was that angel of heaven....the sun, moon, and stars... Sarah.

We both stared at one another, her with a smile and me with a dumfounded expression. She opened her mouth ever so slowly and said, "Greasy Reecey...don't look like it to me that you're goin' to make it to the dance tonight. I guess I'll just have to dance with the other boys in class. Ya know, Boone is real strong and I bet he can just glide over that dance floor. And that Johnny Bodine, well, I am sure could just sweep a girl right off her feet."

I didn't know how to respond. I just stood there and stared at her. My heart – no, my very soul – was crushed. Right then, the door flew open and out came Boone. His head was hung down and he avoided both my and Sarah's gaze.

"Sarah, get back to your chair," Pa said sternly. He motioned me to step into his office. I obeyed, looking back at Boone, who refused to make eye contact. Pa stood by his desk, arms crossed against his chest.

"Look at me son. At the moment... you have two options, but only one choice to make. If you tell me the truth I will not reprimand you. But if you tell me a lie, and I find out about it, there will be hell to pay," he said as he turned around, bent down, and picked up a 12-inch ruler.

As I glanced back out of Pa's office door, I saw Sarah still standing there in the doorway. She had her hand in front of her mouth in an attempt to mask a giggle. Boone stood still, with his head down.

"Reece, think long and hard on it. This is your only chance."

After a few seconds of deliberation, I answered.

"It...it...was me," I replied softly, staring down at the ground.

With a sigh, he said, "Go home. I will meet you there."

"You two," he said, pointing to Sarah and Boone. "Get back to class."

I walked home in somewhat of a daze. I don't remember the route I took. I slumped down on my bed. At the time, I felt that I was the worst son ever. I felt as if I might have lost a father, my best friend, and the girl of my dreams. I lay there feeling sorry for myself until I fell asleep.

ᴄᴌᴏ

"Reece......Reece...will you come down here? NOW!" my father yelled when he arrived home. I sat up and rubbed my eyes, looking out the window. I must have fallen asleep, as the sun was beginning to set.

I slowly walked down the stairs. The screen door was open, and I could see him sitting on the porch bench. An unopened bottle was in his hand. I stared through the open doorway, wary of what may happen.

"Come sit with me?' he said, looking at me. He seemed to be suppressing a smile. As I opened the door and stepped onto the porch, he continued. "You're a good boy most of the time. But you embarrassed the hell out of me today."

"But Pa, I…I didn't mean to. I'm sorry."

With his hands shaking, he put down the unopened bottle. "I know." He stared out into the woods and said softly, "You are so much like her. Do you know that when your mother and I were courting, there was another boy? A boy who was trying to steal her affections away from me?"

"What…what did you do?" I asked, astounded. I had never heard this story before.

17

"Why, I didn't do anything," he said with a smile creeping across his face. "It was your mother. She put two of the biggest crawdads I've ever seen down his pants during a school picnic."

We both started to laugh, the tension washed away. I looked at my father, and for a moment, I could see a light in his eyes as he remembered that day, the happiness of his love for my mother. I wanted to ask him to keep going, to tell me more stories about him and Ma before things changed, when Boone appeared around the corner of the house. Seeing that we were talking, a big grin spread across his face. I could see Caleb trailing behind him, the beginnings of smile on his face, too.

"Hey, Locust Boy," Boone said in a singsong voice. "You got any bugs in your pants?"

"L...L-ocust Boy," repeated Caleb, giggling and shaking his head.

"Sorry, Boone, I mumbled sheepishly. "I didn't mean to get you in trouble. I was just tryin to get Sarah's attention."

Pa let out a whistle. "Boy," Pa said, "there's other ways of getting a girl's attention rather than throwing bugs at her." Another wide grin crossed his face as he took a long drink. "You will go to the dance and apologize to Mary. Boone, you and Caleb make sure he does it proper and all. I have to help with the food and punch," he said, winking at us.

And with that, he stood up and walked inside. I watched him go for a moment before turning back to Boone and Caleb, laughing as they kept teasing and joking around. I wish I could say that I followed him inside, asked him more questions, helped him prepare the food or drinks or...*something*.

But back then I was just a child, a boy of 14, who just wanted to mess around with my friends and get ready for a dance in the hopes of landing the girl of my dreams.

How could I have known?

⤫

About an hour later, after I had cleaned up and changed clothes, Pa, Boone, Caleb, and I headed off to the barnyard dance.

As we rode in the wagon, I asked both Boone and my father who ratted me out about the locusts. Chuckling, Pa said it wasn't Jed or Boone. He explained that a father just knows certain things about his son.

We arrived at Old Man Clover's barn just as the Soak Creek Boys were setting up on the far side. Mr. Clover and his family lived about 10 minutes from town on the main road. His barn, where nearly all of the dancing took place, sat behind the main house in a large field. Mr. Clover had worked all week to lay down fresh straw on the hardwood floor of the barn, which made the wood slightly slippery and smooth. The horses were out to pasture, watched over by one of Mr. Clover's sons. On one side of the barn's front door was a refreshment stand where several of the local ladies served punch, cookies, and elderberry wine. Families were beginning to arrive, and I recognized classmates wandering in and out of the barn.

I also noticed that I was on the receiving end of glances from mothers and fathers, who no doubt heard of my earlier escapade.

Pa pulled the wagon up to a large maple tree and tied up the horse. Boone, Caleb, and I jumped down. Pa turned to face the three of us and said, "Boys, have fun and remember your manners. Each one of you have the goodness of the Lord in your heart."

As we started to stroll up to the barn, he hollered with a slight smile on his face, "Reece…don't forget…you also have to apologize to Mary MacCulcah!"

I must confess that I really didn't look very hard for Ms. MacCulcah as the evening progressed. And soon, apologies for foolish boyhood antics were the furthest thing from my mind.

As we entered the barn, we noticed that most of the people clustered along the right side of the barn and that a small stage had been set up on the opposite side. Several fiddlers were rosining up their bows and two of the men worked to tune up their guitars. Chairs were positioned around the barn where people could sit and talk and it seemed that these were filling up quickly. Some couples began to dance. I saw Jed walking in with his older brother, who immediately went over to talk to one of the members in the band. I noticed that his older brother wore, aside from a hat, a Confederate uniform. Jed wore the hat.

He immediately noticed us and walked over. "Reece, I want you to know that that was a crappy thing you did in class. I didn't mind you doing it, you see, but I do mind you tryin' to pin it on me."

Before I could reply, Boone spoke up. "Jed, quit your squawkin'. Reece planned to confess to his Pa before you got into any real kind of trouble. Weren't you?"

"God's h…h-onest truth Jed," Caleb repeated.

"Shut up, moron," Jed snapped back at Boone. "You and Caleb would stick up for him if he got caught red-handed robbing old man Haskin's store."

"Would not," Boone shot back.

"Would too," Jed said.

"Would not."

"Would too."

"Jed." I interrupted, "tell you what. I'll make it up to you."

"How?" he asked suspiciously.

Thinking quickly, I said, 'Well...the next time I go turkey hunting, I'll give my first bird to you."

"No way," he scoffed. "I don't have much taste for turkey. I want your good knife, the one your Pa gave you."

"My Mumblety-Peg knife?' I replied. My one and only Mumblety-Peg knife. It was one of my favorite gifts from Pa. "Old Timber?"

"Yep," he said with an ornery smile. "That'd be the one."

Boone and Caleb stared at me with eyes wide. No boy of that age would give away his one true companion, his protector in time of need, his precious Excalibur.

I thought for a moment, trying to figure out a way to weasel out of this when the band started in with a rousing rendition of "The Bonnie Blue Flag."

Jed whooped for joy and immediately turned around and started to laugh and do a jig. "Woooo BOY, hold on to my cap, Reece my boy, I got' a dance to this one!" As he grabbed the nearest girl and proceeded to the dance floor, he looked back at me and yelled over the music, "Think it over!"

Laughing, I put his cap on.

"We Are A Band OF Brothers And Native To The Soil
Fighting For Our Liberty, With Treasure, Blood, And Toil
And When Our Rights Were Threatened,
The Cry Rose Near And Far
Hurrah For The Bonnie Blue Flag That Bears A Single Star
Hurrah!! Hurrah!! For Southern Rights, Hurrah!!
Hurrah For The Bonnie Blue Flag That Bears A Single Star"

I smiled as I watched most of the crowd dance and sing; however, there were some sitting down obviously displeased with the choice of song. It was then that I glanced over to the two large entry doors at the front of the barn and saw Sarah and her family entering. She was followed minutes later by a large, well-decorated Union Officer.

No one seemed to take notice as everyone appeared to be caught up in their own revelry.

"Oh, cripes!' I muttered under my breath. Most people in the town of Cucumber kept their opinions about the current conflict to themselves. But there were a few, on both sides (such as Jed's family), who openly displayed their pleasure or displeasure at the current rebellion.

The Union Officer was followed by three of his men. They stood by the officer, leering at those who were dancing.

Boone slowly shoved Caleb behind him and, leaning over, whispered to me. "The officer's name is Colonel Jacob 'Black Damp' McCabe. Ol' Black Damp is the meanest cuss this side of Richmond."

It was at this moment people in the crowd and those dancing took notice of the newest guests. The music slowly started to fade and came to a stop altogether. The room became eerily quiet.

You could hear a pin drop.

"Well, well, well, what do we have here?" jeered Black Damp. "A bunch of SOUTHERN SYMPATHIZERS dancing and singing to the cause! Sergeant, I do believe that we need to teach these vermin a lesson."

He slowly withdrew his sabre.

Before I could even process what was happening, I saw Pa walk over to him and speak up. "Colonel, sir, with all due respect, these people were just letting off a little steam. These are trying times, with families having sent their fathers and sons off to war on both sides of this conflict."

Black Damp looked at my father and an unnatural smile slowly spread across his face. "Bullshit," he hissed.

And then he plunged his sword deep into my father's belly.

CHAPTER 4

A Promise Made

Since the war began, Colonel Jacob McCabe was in the thick of it. For the most part, he never really served under any one command. He, more or less, took matters into his own hands. Given the nickname "Black Damp" after the black coal filth found underground, it is said that most of his troops came from the jails and mental institutions of towns that he so-called "liberated." During the year of 1863, he killed and butchered more women and children in the Appalachians than the Yellow Fever outbreak in 1855, which killed over 3,000 people.

And one of those was the one person that meant the most to me.

After Black Damp murdered my Pa, everything seemed to move in slow motion. I hardly recall what happened. I remember yelling out, "NO...PA!" and trying to run to him, but Boone, Caleb, and Jed grabbed me and pushed me through a side door. I heard screams and yelling inside the barn, followed by a cascade of gunshots. I remember my cries and wails. My father, my hero, the one who guided me in life, who never would do harm to another person and loved all mankind, whose joy in life was to mentor and teach all who would listen, was gone, all in the blink of an eye.

I was told some time later that Boone and Caleb put me in the back of the wagon and placed a blanket over me. We moved quickly to the house, loaded up food, clothes, and hunting rifles, and left town.

The two days immediately following remain a blur. I cried, slept, cried, and slept some more. I think I was in shock. I felt as if my soul, my being, my very essence was forever damaged. I could feel a change in me that I couldn't wrap my mind around. Sitting in the back of that wagon, I didn't know where we were going, but I did know that sometime in the future, I would come for him, and do unforgivable things, no matter how horrible. I wished to stray into his dreams. I vowed that I would kill Colonel Jacob "Black Damp" McCabe and all who got in my way. I would not only kill him but I would kill his family, his wife and children (if the monster had any). I would destroy all that he owns. If that meant for me to die in the process, so be it. If that meant for me to go to hell, then I will make sure he goes with me.

I renounced my Quaker upbringing. It now became the religion of my past. The pursuit of my retribution was my future.

Ↄↄ

The afternoon was fading on about the third day when I final snapped out of it. I don't know how or why, but something hit me and I became instantly aware of my surroundings. Boone drove the wagon and Caleb sat beside him, munching on an apple. I sat there, not knowing what to say, when Boone spoke up. How he knew I was awake, I'll never know.

"We're on a back road headin' to Lewisburg. From there we're fixin' to go to Richmond to hook up with the 22nd Virginia Regiment out of Charleston."

"What? How do you know they'll be there?" I asked as I shook my head, trying to comprehend what he was talking about.

"Well," he replied, "while we were leading you out of the barn, Jed told me that's who all the local boys signed with. Jed said that he would meet up with us on the third day at Old Sam Black Church."

After several minutes of silence, Boone muttered under his breath. "Reece...Caleb and I want to kill that bastard." With his head bowed, Caleb said nothing. I could see tears in his eyes as he stared straight ahead. Boone sighed, and glanced back at me for a moment before looking away. "Your Pa may have taken to the drink from time to time, but he was always fair and kind to both of us."

After that, we rode in silence, each of us lost in our own thoughts. Every time I thought about my father, tears would threaten to stream down my face. I didn't want them to see, so I made sure that I faced the back of the wagon, looking towards the back of the road as we slowly made our way east.

Sometime later, we slowed down and stopped. I turned around and saw an old, burned-out church on the side of the road with a small graveyard in the back. The sun was beginning to set, and as I jumped down from the wagon, I noticed Boone and Caleb standing very still, staring at the church. Feeling uneasy, I reached in the wagon and pulled out my rifle. I thought that maybe we might run into Black Damp or one of his men, and I wanted to be ready.

But it was not Black Damp nor any of his men.

As I walked around the right side of the wagon, I noticed smoke from a small campfire coming from the left side of the church and the graveyard. I pointed towards the direction of the fire, and Boone and Caleb reached into the wagon bed and pulled out their rifles, too.

Boone motioned me to go right and whispered to Caleb to stay here and get in the wagon. He then started slowly creeping left. As we got closer to the church, a loud voice boomed out behind us.

"BOYS.....HALT right there! Don't be turning' around neither or I'll DROP YOU like a bag of DIRT!"

Boone and I wheeled around at the same time, and about 10 yards behind us was an older man sitting on a white and grey horse. He had a gnarled beard and was dressed in a long, unbuttoned overcoat. What looked like a ten-dollar gold piece dangled from a chain around his neck. He pointed a rifle at Boone with his left hand and a pistol at me in his right.

Chuckling, he said, "Looks like I got a jump on you two." He slowly got down from his horse, never taking his eyes off us.

"You boys friend or foe?" he asked, dropping his voice a little.

"Depends," I said, quickly glancing over at Boone.

"Well," he said, "you all sure don't look like no Yankees…
but neither do you like no Rebs. Now… slowly drop those
toothpicks and well sort this out true and true."

Suddenly, a voice rang out from behind him. Actually, it
was more of a choked screech than a yell. "M…m-ister…I
got you dead in my s…s-sights and I ain't afraid to blow your
brains out! Drop your weapons or prepare to dddie…er get
killed in a most horrible w…w-ay!"

Caleb.

The man looked stunned for a moment, and then slowly
a smile spread across his weathered face. It was then, as he
bent down to drop his guns, that I noticed a bloodstain in
the middle of his shirt.

"Well, you boys sure got a drop on me. Didn't see the kid
in the wagon."

"Be quiet!" I snapped. "If you're a damn Yankee, then we're
gonna string you up and leave your carcass to rot in the wind!"
Letting that sink in for a couple of seconds, I continued.
"And…if you're in Black Damp McCabe's outfit, then we're
gonna skewer your liver and feed it to the buzzards…all while
you watch and rot!"

Not taking his eyes off me, the old man motioned to
Boone. "Take the saddlebag off my horse and you'll find a tin
box with the words *To Frenchie* on the lid." Boone did as he
was instructed. Meanwhile, Caleb climbed out of the wagon
and stood behind me.

As Boone walked over to the horse, I attempted to stare
this man down. "Sit down by the wagon and do it real slow,"
I hissed, keeping my rifle pointed at his chest.

"Reeaaal slow," repeated Caleb.

The man walked over to the wagon and turned to face me. As he sat, his face winced and he moaned softly in pain as he grabbed his stomach. It was then that Boone walked over with the saddlebag and a tin box. Sure enough, it had the exact words inscribed on the lid.

The man forced a smile and said, "Open it up, son." Boone did as he was instructed and pulled out a piece of paper.

"Read it," he said.

> *To Captain George S. Patton:*
>
> *Having been captured, wounded, and left on the field in the Battle of Scary Creek, Virginia; and having taken a solemn oath that you will never take up arms against this United States Government again under penalty of death, you hereby have been granted full immunity from all prosecution and are entitled to live out the remaining portion of your life quietly and under all perpetuity.*
>
> *Signed,*
>
> *Major General Jacob D. Cox, Kanawha Division XXIII Corp United States Army.*

"Who's Frenchie?" I asked.

"That's me. It's what my wife calls me," said the man, somewhat embarrassed. He looked at me for a moment before letting out a long sigh. "Now what?"

Boone grinned, looked at me, then at Caleb and said, "Let's eat!"

CHAPTER 5

The Meeting

Caleb and I gently led the Captain to his campfire and propped him up beside an old Oak Tree. However, as the Captain sat down, Caleb proceeded to stand over him and unbutton his britches.

"What the hell?" yelped the Captain as he tried to scurry away. However, Caleb's legs straddled his body and prevented him from doing so.

"We gots to p...p-eeee on you." exclaimed Caleb, matter-of-factly. "Urination is a natural medicine."

"Whoa...wait just a minute here..." replied the Captain, who was still trying to scuttle away.

I looked at Boone and chuckled. Boone shook his head and put it in his hands with a loud sigh. "Caleb," I replied gently but firmly. "No one's going to pee on anyone. Find me some Dandelion and Pokeweed to make some wild tea." I looked at the Captain. "It might ease your pain."

"Jesus…was that kid serious?" he asked as Caleb hitched up his pants and scooted away. I turned my head away without answering, not wanting either one to see the laughter on my face.

"Boone, I said, "make sure that the fire is small. We don't want any blue-bellies to come riding up. Then go get the wagon and bring it to the back of the church. Get out some potatoes and tack. We'll make him a thick broth for dinner."

I tore open the Captain's shirt which revealed a small hole about one-inch above his belly button. The wound did not appear too deep, as it had mostly scarred over. I did notice, however, that there was some crusted puss around the edges and the skin was purple and red.

With his right hand, the Captain tugged at the chain gold piece around his neck. He held it up for me to see. The middle part of the coin was bent inward and discolored. "Damn thing saved my life," he said, looking at it. "The ball hit right in the middle of the coin and drove both into my stomach about two inches."

"God Damn Yankees," I replied. 'We're on our way to join the militia in Richmond."

"They're not there," he said, looking back up at me. "They have orders to go to Lewisburg to stop General Averell's attack on the railroad."

"Oh," I muttered, unsure of what to say. 'Um…. good. We'll sign up there."

"Listen," he said, narrowing his eyes a bit as he inspected me. "I don't mean to be mindin' your business, but you boys seem to be a might young and all. Where your folks?"

Tears starting forming in my eyes and I turned away. I stood up and walked to the fire without another word. As I stared at the smoke disappearing into the night sky, I heard the Captain whisper softly, "I'm sorry."

Caleb returned with the weeds, and I crushed both herbs and mixed in the water. I threw in the potatoes and waited for the broth to boil. Meanwhile, Boone hid the wagon behind the church and tied his horse to the same oak tree he was lying beside. Soon the broth came to a boil, and I poured it into a tin cup. I took this and some hard tack to the Captain.

"You boys don't happen to have any liquor, do ya? I'm a might parched an all…strictly for medicinal purposes, you see," the Captain said, taking a sip from the broth and making a face.

"Caleb, go get that ole' rot gut whiskey that's been in the wagon," instructed Boone. Caleb did so and returned immediately with a full bottle.

The Captain took a deep swig. "Hot damn, that's good. Just what I needed!" he said, smiling.

The three of us then sat beside him and started to eat. The Captain spoke first.

"So, what's your names?' he asked. I watched him sip the whisky and pour out the tea.

"This here's Caleb and Boone. They're brothers and my best friends,' I replied, motioning to them. "My name is Reece. We come from about 30 miles west near Beckleyville called Cucumber. 'We….ah…have no family to speak of."

"You mentioned Black Damp,' the Captain said, looking at his whiskey. Then he looked up and straight at me. "We've been tryin' to put a stop to him and his kind since the war broke out, but he always seems one step ahead. He's a son of a bitch, alright. He don't seem to want to fight out in the open. He's more of a marauder-vigilante type. Cowards all."

"Captain," said Boone, "are you really out of the war, so to speak? Your papers write like you gave up. That true?"

"Well," he said steadily, "you're right. If I am caught, there's a sure bet I'll be hanged."

"But," he continued, flashing us a sly grin, "they gotta catch me first."

⚙

It was getting late, and the fire had died down. The Captain had told us stories about the various battles he had been in, his family back in Charleston, before beginning to nod off here and there. Boone and I looked at one another and agreed that he would take the first watch, and me the next.

"Caleb," I whispered before laying down, "sleep near him, and if he wakes up, give him the tea. Keep him away from the whiskey."

As the quarter moon slowly rose from the east for the next few hours, all was relatively quiet. As I tried to sleep, I looked up at the night sky, and above the graveyard, several shooting stars raced by. About an hour after I relieved Boone, as a thick fog settled over the tombstones, I caught glimpse of the soft glow of torchlights ahead, far off in the distance. I immediately put out what was left of the campfire. The lights were visible for about 15 minutes, and then drifted out of sight. I heard wolves howling about an hour later, and then all was eerily quiet for the remainder of the night. At some point I was relieved by Caleb and as my head hit the ground I immediately drifted off, the day's exhaustion finally enveloping me like a blanket.

The first light of day had not yet climbed over the mountains when I woke. I was thinking of my father when I saw Boone get up and go relieve himself in the woods. After a few minutes, he came back and covered Caleb with a blanket that he had kicked off some time in the night. I looked over at Captain Patton – he was sound asleep breathing softly. For a moment, I remembered the torchlights during watch, but quickly forgot about them when I smelled coffee brewing on the fire.

I got up and checked on the horses and wagon and all appeared to be safe. When I got back, the Captain had woken and was sipping a mug of coffee that Boone had given him.

Not wanting to wake up Caleb, Captain Patton whispered to both Boone and I. "I know you boys have been through a lot. I know your belly aches for revenge. But I want to make this very clear. Soldiering, war, and all that goes with it plays with a man's soul. It sucks out the very essence from a person. Once you go through with it you will never….*ever*…be the same. Do you understand?"

Boone and I glanced at each other and muttered yes. "Me too," replied Caleb, yawning and sitting up as he rubbed his eyes. "I understand t…t-too."

The Captain stood up gingerly, bracing himself with the trunk of the tree. He motioned to Caleb. "Caleb, my boy, go fetch me that bottle I was partaking of last night."

34

Caleb stood there for a moment, looking at him, then at both of us. "Go on Caleb, it'll be alright,' I said. Caleb walked over to the wagon and returned with the bottle.

The Captain took a long, hard drink, and then started walking into the graveyard. The three of us trailed behind, exchanging looks. Suddenly, the Captain stopped and turned to face us. 'Okay, I feel your desire for payback. But first, you all need to be able to load and shoot your guns twice… within one minute…all while being fired upon."

He drank the remaining whiskey from the bottle and set it down about 50 yards from us on top of an old, weathered gravestone. He turned around and faced us, pulling out a pistol that was hidden behind his back.

Damn him. He was as sly as a fox. He had it all this time.

He pointed the pistol at us and yelled for me to put down my tin of tea on a small stump which was about two feet from my left. He gave a lopsided grin and yelled, "Go boys, fetch your rifles! Load 'em up and on my command, shoot the bottle."

We went to the wagon and retrieved our rifles. All three guns were already loaded. We walked back and lined up, aiming our rifles at the bottle.

"Ready….aim….FIRE!' the Captain yelled out.

The guns bellowed out a haze of gun powder. All three of us missed. As I dropped my weapon to reload, the Captain fired his pistol and the tin cup bounced off the stump and rolled next to my leg.

"AGAIN!' he yelled as he stumbled forward towards us, pistol raised and eyes wide

I glanced over at Boone in shock. His mouth was wide open.

The Captain fired again, hitting the cup once more. This time the cup fell between my legs. Looking down, I took a deep breath and tried to concentrate on reloading my rifle. I heard a thump between my legs and the tin cup flew up and over my right leg.

Caleb fainted.

Quickly finishing, I looked up just in time to see his pistol pointed inches from my head.

Boone had his hands up, surrendering.

I raised my rifle, fired, and shattered the bottle resting on the tombstone behind the Captain. He lowered his weapon and shook his head as he looked at the three of us. "Jesus, at least one of ya can shoot." He turned and as he walked back towards the fire he said "It ain't just about all this," he said waving his hand around.

"Wha….what do you mean? I replied turning and watching him go.

He paused just for a moment and facing the fire replied "It's…just… that you've got to live with it."

ᄽ

In the afternoon on the fourth day, Captain Patton said we needed to travel towards Lewisburg. We still had not seen any sign of Jed. Not wanting to leave our friend behind, we left a note beside the campfire saying that we were headed toward Lewisburg and to meet us there. We figured if any Yankees found the note, we would be well on our way.

Boone, Caleb, and I loaded the supplies in the wagon and the Captain, ever-so-slowly, climbed up on his horse and we proceeded down the trail.

We weren't five minutes into our journey when the three of us saw something leaving from the edge of the Valley of Thorns onto the road ahead. The Five Finger Mountains came closest to the road at this point and were about five miles north. Whatever it was, it was about 400 yards from us, weaving and faltering erratically. I stood on the wagon to get a better view and saw that it was a horse. It appeared to be covered in blood and the saddle was tilted off to the side as if the rider had been pulled away.

"We need to shoot it. Looks like it may have rabies," said the Captain, staring intently at the poor creature. "Reece, you're standing on the wagon. Take the shot."

I stood on top of the bucket seat and nestled my gun against my shoulder. Taking careful aim, I gently squeezed the trigger and felt the kick of the rifle. Staring ahead, I saw the horse fall and lay still on the ground. As we carefully approached I recognized the horse. It was Jed's.

It did not have rabies.

Deep claw marked had opened its belly, and the saddle which was positioned on the side of the horse had prevented the intestines from falling out. Small bite marks were all over its body. It was a small wonder that it had made it this far alive. The most disturbing thing, however, was that the thick leather saddle had a six-inch claw mark running across the side.

The saddle was nearly clawed in half.

The Captain, a few feet ahead of us, let out a low whistle. Boone looked at me for a moment before looking away, and we rode by the horse without a word passed amongst us. I swallowed down the bile rising in my throat.

After about an hour, we ran into the main road going to Lewisburg. Looking out for bushwhackers, we started heading east.

We saw the first black and white turkey vulture about midday.

The sun beat down directly overhead. As we rounded a bend in the road, there, halfway up an old pine tree, was Jed.

Well, what was left of him.

CHAPTER 6
Our Arrival

At early evening on the fourth day of our journey east, we buried my friend Jed Williams. Boone and I shimmied up an old pine tree where he was skewered – his upper torso impaled on a tree branch, and his lower body gone, almost as if it had been ripped away. The two of us gently lowered him to the ground. From the wagon, the Captain retrieved a blanket to cover him up.

The three of us just stared at the body, not saying anything.

I spoke up first. "Sons of bitches." Boone and Caleb muttered in agreement. Boone replied, matter-of-fact, "First dead body I've ever seen and it have to be a friend."

"Boone!" yelled the Captain, who had wandered away, down the trail. "There's a small knoll over there 'bout 20 yards away. Wrap his body in the blanket and lay it over there."

We did as we were told, carrying his body over to the small clearing.

"We don't have any shovels, so we need to cover his body with stones," the Captain said. No one moved. We just kept staring at Jed.

"REECE! BOONE! Do as I say…NOW! There's going to be a lot more than that in the hell that we're headin!"

The Captain's voice shook me out of the spell I was under. I turned from the body, fighting back tears as I wiped my brow with my arm. I took a deep breath, and touched the cap on my head.

Jed's cap.

For the next couple of hours, we scoured the immediate area, looking for stones. Curiously, we saw no one else on the trail. We seldom spoke, each absorbed in our own thoughts. As dusk descended, we finally found enough stones to cover Jed's entire body. The Captain fashioned a crude wooden cross from the sideboard of the wagon and carved Jed's full name onto one of the pieces. With one of the pieces of stone, we hammered the makeshift cross into the ground.

As we stared down at the grave, the Captain muttered under his breath. "Give up, my ass." After a short pause, he again muttered, more to himself than to us. "He was just a kid."

After several minutes, he knelt down on both knees and prayed softly. I strained to make out the words:

You there. So, I see my Father.
You there. So, I see my Mother, and my sister and brothers.
You there. So, I see my people back to the beginning of time.
The Lord has called on me.

*So please take his body as we have placed it in a shallowed
grave where his soul can reach the halls of heaven and where
the brave can live forever.*
Amen.

I took Jed's cap off my head and placed it on the stones.
"Rest easy, my friend."

❧

As the night began to close in, we decided to travel a little
further. A nearly-full moon was riding the horizon sky and we
could easily see the road without much difficulty. After some
time, headed down the other side of a rather steep mountain,
we spied campfires spread along the valley below, dozens of
small, orange dots scattered across the basin.

"The road is straight and narrow, neither curving right
nor left," explained the Captain. "We must proceed quietly."

"Hear that Caleb?' whispered Boone. "Quietly."

"Shut up, Boone,' snapped Caleb.

Boone replied, a little louder, "You shut up, Caleb.'

Caleb responded, this time much louder, "You SHUT
UP BOONE!"

"Jesus! Would you both SHUT UP?" hissed the Captain.

As we rode in silence, I looked down at that the valley
below, spread as far as my eyes could see. Campfires blazed
on both sides of the Greenbrier River and in the distance,
beyond the farthest campfires, were the lights of Lewisburg.

As we reached the bottom of the mountain, the nearest
campfire glowed only about a half a mile away. Caption Patton
turned to us and whispered, "We have a hard decision to

41

make. As far as I can tell, it appears that the Union troops are positioned on this side of the river. We can try to ride past 'em in the night over Walker's Bridge, or we can hide the wagon in a group of trees and cross the river with the horses about a mile upstream. Either way, we're takin' a big risk."

Boone and I looked at one another. "Reece…Caleb can't swim," said Boone softly, his voice wavering. "Boone," I replied, looking him in the eyes, "there's bound to be plenty of sentries on the bridge. If the Captain could lead the horses, I'll take the rifles and what little supplies we have and you can carry Caleb on your back."

The Captain agreed to the plan. The four of us veered off the trail when it bent left, and I unhooked the horse and drove the wagon into a thicket of briars and brush. *At least any Yankees trying to take the wagon will have hell to pay with all these prickles and thorns*, I thought. Meanwhile, the Captain climbed down from his horse and tied both reigns across his waist. Ever so quietly, we crept to the riverbank.

We slinked forward single file. The Captain took the lead and guided the horses, followed by Boone with Caleb on his back. I followed last – if Caleb fell off, Boone and I hoped that I would have a chance of catching him before he drifted away.

As the Captain stepped in the water, he sank down to his chest. The horses followed immediately. They seemed to enjoy the coolness of the water. Boone entered next, slipping slightly. I could see Caleb hanging on for dear life with his hands wrapped around Boone's neck.

"Caleb, Caleb!' whispered Boone loudly. 'Relax. Relax! Wrap your hands around my shoulders." Caleb turned his head frantically back towards me. "I'm here, Caleb,' I whispered as I looked him in the eyes. "If you fall, I got ya."

We prayed that the sound of the river would drown out any noise we made during crossing, and every now and then, the Captain would stop and listen for any noise along both the bank and the bridge. Being nearly a full moon, I thought that any fool of a Yank could see us, but apparently all eyes were turned toward the town.

After what felt like an eternity, we finally arrived on the other side of the river. We wearily climbed up the bank and after several minutes of rest, we traveled onward.

Toward what...we did not know.

CHAPTER 7

Patton's Rangers

Barely 10 minutes after we resumed our journey, we heard the all-too familiar "Halt! Who goes there?"

I froze immediately, my heart leaping out of my chest. The Captain hesitated only for a moment before letting out a laugh. "Tom!" he yelled into the darkness. "Is that you?"

For a moment, all was quiet. Then the voice hollered back. "…Cap?"

"Yes, it's me, Tom! Lower your rifles. We're comin' through."

After a pause, a second voice chimed in. "Hold on a minute, how we to know that you're the *real* Cap' Patton? Captain Patton was shot in the belly at the battle of Scary Creek. I was there when he was mortally wounded."

Under his breath, the Captain cursed. "Goddamn you, Bill Ford, you must be drunk again!' he shouted back.

Another pause. "If you're the REAL Cap' Patton, what's the love name that your wife calls you?"

"WHY YOU FOUL BREATH SON OF A MULE!" yelled the Captain. "How'd you know 'bout that?" He sighed, and then somewhat reluctantly yelled, "FRENCHIE!"

We heard some muffled whispers and laughter, and after a minute or two, the first voice called out, "Okay. Come on up, slowly."

We marched up the hill in single file. We were still dripping wet and I am sure when the two sentries caught glimpse of us, we looked more like a bunch of wet fish than soldiers. When we arrived at the top of the embankment, we spotted a small campfire glow. Two men pointed their rifles towards us. When they saw Captain Patton, however, both lowered their weapons and slowly saluted.

"At ease, soldiers. Good to see you boys," instructed Captain Patton with a grin.

Both men stared with wide eyes. "Cap...is that really you?" asked one of the men, as if not believing his eyes.

"Tom, it's good to see you. How's Elly and the children?" replied the Captain. Both men ran up to us, and one of them gave the Captain a big bear hug.

"Damn good to see you," said he said, wiping his eyes. "They're fine. When Elly and the kids heard you was dead, why, I don't think..." he trailed off.

"Tom, it's alright. I'm here now."

The soldier brightened up and beamed. "Yes sir, yes sir, why you surely are."

The other sentry stood wide-eyed with disbelief. He looked us up and down and murmured under his breath, "Good Lord, you fellers are nothin' but a bunch of tadpoles."

Looking at our wet clothes, he said, "Come sit by the fire and skinny out of them wet britches. I'll go get some extra clothes from the supply tent and be right back."

As he ran towards the scattered campfires, we heard him yell, "Captain…Caption Patton is back. The ole coot is alive!"

We all walked over to the campfire to get warm. The Captain slapped Tom on the back and smiled. "Boys," he said to us, "welcome to Patton's Rangers. I want you to meet Sergeant Tom Hatfield. The best goddam soldier in this here outfit."

"Boys, it's good to meet you. Cap says you fellers have had a time of it," Sergeant Hatfield said, extending his hand to shake ours one-by-one.

"Yes sir," I replied, shaking his hand. I motioned to Boone and Caleb. "This here is Boone and Caleb. My name is Reece. We've come to join up and kill us some Yankees."

He smiled. "Well, you've come to the right place, alright. If you don't mind me asking…how old are you boys?"

I paused and glanced over to Boone. "Well… Caleb and I are…ahh…16."

Taking my cue Boone, blurted out, "Ahhh….I'm 18."

The Sergeant and the Captain looked at us, amused. "Well, if the Captain vouches for you all, let's get some clean uniforms and some food in your bellies."

Meanwhile, other soldiers started showing up at the campfire, and it seemed almost like a family reunion for Captain Patton. Men took turns slapping him on the back, offering up hot coffee, biscuits, and hardtack. After a bit, a thin-looking Lieutenant sporting a long blonde ponytail tied at the end with a red ribbon walked up to him. He immediately swooped off his feathered hat and nervously presented himself with a rather large and flashy bow.

"First Lieutenant Henri` Dumont at your service, Monsieur."

All three of us stopped what we were doing and stared at this man. We had never really heard anyone like this speak in such a way.

Boone leaned over to me and whispered, "Who is this…?" However, before he could finish his sentence, the Lieutenant turned to us and once again proceeded to extravagantly swoop his hat low to the ground and bow.

"Tom, what happed to Beau? He's in charge of my cavalry. Who is this mockingjay?" Captain Patton said gruffly, looking the Lieutenant up and down.

"Cap, Beau was killed two days ago just south of here," Tom said quietly, before looking down for a moment. He raised his head and coughed. "Sir, may I present First Lieu-tenant Henri` Dumont from the great state of Louisiana. The Yankees call him the "Ragin' Cajun." He's a damn fine cavalry officer – was Captain Washburn's second-in-command.

It wasn't until much later that we learned more about Lieutenant Dumont. In the beginning of the war, Dumont was one of the best light cavalry officers of the south. He was heroic and dashing on horseback, and it is said that during the Battle of the First Manassas the young cavalry officer led the counterattack ordered by General Thomas "Stonewall" Jackson, which turned the tide of battle in favor of the Confederacy. His assault was so bold that one Union General didn't even have time to get on his horse. The

General, it is said, presented his sabre as a formal declaration of surrender; however, First Lieutenant Dumont did not accept this prize. Instead, Dumont removed a red ribbon from the General's waist which happened to be a gift from the General's daughter.'

The "Ragin Cajun" always wore this around his ponytail as a trophy for good luck.

Bill came back, muttering apologies for the uniforms. The outfits he found, except for Boone's, were all too large. I noticed that the belt for my uniform was blood stained, and that the jacket that Caleb wore was torn at the shoulder.

Nevertheless, finally, we felt like we belonged.

I then overheard the Captain talking to Sergeant Hatfield. "Tom," he asked in a hushed voice, "what's the situation? Where're William's troops at?"

"Sir," replied the Sergeant, "General Averell has scattered his troops across the river from ours for about five miles. He's got us outmanned by about five to one. I figure in two days' time, he will cross the river at Walker's Bridge, march right into Lewisburg and blow us to bits with his 20 pounders."

"Goddamnit," cursed the Captain. "Sergeant, send a message to General Echols that I am back and alive. Tell him that with his permission, we will all be leaving here at first light and head north. At least well lead 'em away from town."

The Captain sighed and rubbed his temple. He turned to face Lieutenant Dumont. "You...ah...Dumont. You are the very eyes of what's left of my goddamn cavalry. I need you and your command to ride before first light towards Droop Mountain. Now, listen carefully. About a mile before The

Droop starts to rise, bear left and go into... ah... what you boys call that place?" the Captain said, turning to face us.

"The Five Finger Mountains," replied Boone, still staring in amazement at the First Lieutenant.

"That's right. General Averell thinks he has us pinned between the town, the river, and Droop Mountain. We're gonna go up the Ole' Droop tomorrow morning and he's gonna follow."

Captain Patton gave an icy stare to the First Lieutenant.

"And when he gets to the middle of that shithole of a mountain you, sir, are going to leave the Five Finger Mountains and attack him from below and ram my cavalry up his ass!"

The trap had been set. Captain Patton turned from the First Lieutenant and locked eyes with the Sergeant.

"You give a Yankee General a cookie...and he's gonna want a glass of milk."

'Yes, sir!' saluted the Sergeant. As he was barking the orders, the Captain turned toward us and smiled gently. "You boys. This is where we have to part. You'll be in good hands. Get some rest tonight because we move out at dawn."

"Yes sir. Captain, thank you for all you've done getting us here," I said, shaking his hand.

The Captain smiled again and looked at the three of us. "You stay safe!" he instructed as he turned and began to walk away. "And remember.... shoot straight!" he yelled back with a grin.

And with that, he was gone.

Boone, Caleb, and I wandered further into the campsite, taking in all the smells and sights of our newfound army.

I found a small open area near a fire, and the three of us finally laid ourselves down. The day's events finally catching up with us, we immediately went to sleep. I closed my eyes and thought of Pa. My retribution was at hand. It was so close that I could taste it. I fell asleep with a smile of satisfaction on my face.

And several hours later, in the dead of sleep, we were shaken awake and told to gather our gear to leave.

CHAPTER 8

The Dandy

One of the nearby men walked up to us and said we could march with him and his companions. He asked where we were from, and after replying that we were from Cucumber, his eyes brightened and he said he was from nearby Beckleyville. He introduced himself as Jack Hinson, however he told us he goes by the name "Old Jack."

He glanced at Boone and Caleb. "You boy's brothers?" he asked, looking them up and down. Before Boone or Caleb could reply, he looked down at the ground and said softly, "They executed my two boys. They suspected them of being bushwhackers." He looked away. He seemed lost in his thoughts for a moment, then he turned back to us. He gave us a slight smile "I'm going to raise me a ruckus. Me and my Lucy Sue," he said, looking at his Kentucky Long Rifle. "If they're within 500 yards, I plan to pick off the officers, one-by-one."

About that time, Sergeant Hatfield arrived carrying three .58 Caliber percussion cap rifles. "Dump those pea shooters and try these on for size," he said, tossing them to us. All three had been outfitted with shoulder straps and bayonet clips. The rifle that was given to me had four notches on the side of the wooden shoulder stock.

It was apparent that all three had been used before.

The Sergeant also provided us with two revolvers and one oversized Bowie knife. Boone immediately grabbed the Bowie knife, muttering something about now really having the advantage in Mumblety-Peg. Both Caleb and I took the pistols. We tucked them under our belts and proceeded to fall in line.

The early morning light had just begun to erase the night when we started our march north. We began our trek the same time that First Lieutenant Dumont (still sporting that long, flamboyant ponytail tied back with the red ribbon) and the 20th Virginia Cavalry broke camp. Every quarter mile rode an officer, and riders bearing messages would travel up and back along the column, bringing messages from the First Lieutenant. Every so often, we would stop and rest for around 30 minutes or so, and were allowed to go to the nearest supply wagon to get water.

It was getting hot by the afternoon. We marched past a handful of soldiers resting beside a cannon when a horse and rider approached. The rider urged his mount to stop and, without any apparent reason, started yelling at the resting men.

"You LAZY, NO GOOD, SONS of a MOTHER'S WHORE. Get your ASSES UP and GET MOVIN!"

The rider appeared to be a boy not much older than us on horseback, wearing the most vulgar and brazen uniform that I had ever laid eyes on. His cap had two oversized red feathers sticking out from the back, and along his top coat, he wore a red scarf which draped down across his saddle. The coat was Confederate gray with stripes trailing down the sleeves and pants. He had a pistol tucked into his front waistband along with a long sabre. The sabre was much too long for the boy – he would have to dismount in order to unsheathe the thing.

Boone and I took one look and started laughing. We couldn't help ourselves. The more we laughed, the more others around us began to laugh. Pretty soon the officers nearby also started laughing. The boy turned bright red in the face. He turned the horse around and rode up to face us.

"Well…well…what have we here?" he sneered, looking down at us. 'I do tell I see nothing but a bunch of huckleberries. Why, I didn't know they made 'em so small back at the farm."

Not wanting to get in trouble, Boone and I turned away, still chuckling. "Come back, boy!" snarled the boy on horseback. Turning back, I looked up and he had taken out the pistol.

He pointed it right at me.

I stared up. I put my arms out to show that I had no weapon except the pistol tucked in the holster. My rifle was slung across my back. The other soldiers frantically looked around and starting taking backward steps until there was a small ring around us. I did not see Boone or Caleb.

The boy slowly smiled and cocked the pistol. I remember thinking, *hell, I just joined this outfit and am already in trouble.* I didn't want to lose face to this dandy. Not taking my eyes off the boy, I replied ever so slowly, "I didn't mean no disrespect. We are on the same side, you and me."

"Don't think so. I think I am gonna put this here bullet right between your eyes."

"Well then,' I replied, never taking my eyes off of his face. "Get your ass down and make it fair. Just you and me."

"Reece!" snapped Boone, who had stepped up from the crowd, "Watch his other hand! He's got another pistol behind his back!" Before the boy could draw out the second pistol, I quickly jerked left and then right, nudging and startling the boy's horse. The horse jolted, causing the boy to fire the gun.

The bullet missed my head by a matter of inches.

The boy immediately lost his balance and fell off the saddle, a heavy thud hitting the ground. Someone in the crowd grabbed the horse's reigns while I quickly drew my pistol, aiming it down at the boy on the ground.

"HOLD IT RIGHT THERE!" rang out a familiar voice. I looked over and saw Captain Patton with two of his adjutants riding up. Not turning my back to the boy, I stepped back slightly. The boy stood up and hissed softly, "Next time, I'll gut you like a deer."

I stared directly in his eyes and replied, "Just you and me…real soon."

He smirked. "My knife will slice through you like warm butter."

"That's ENOUGH, Lawrence!" the Captain snapped as he rode up. "Get back on your horse and follow the supply wagons where you're supposed to be." He turned and looked at me. "Reece, you and your boys okay?'

"Yes sir," I replied, looking back at the boy. He climbed back on his horse and before he turned to go, he looked at me and made a slash across his neck with his thumb. He pulled hard on the reigns and the horse reared, and he galloped away screeching the rebel yell.

"That'd be my nephew, Lawrence Perceval Rutherford III," moaned the Captain, shaking his head left to right. "My sister-in-law's son. Promised her I'd watch over him. He'll be the death of me yet, the spoiled little brat. Sorry you had to run into him." He sighed again, rubbing his brow wearily.

One of the officers beside the Captain cleared his throat and said, "Sir, we have not received any messages from the Caj...er, the First Lieutenant for several hours." Captain Patton frowned for a moment, then looked back at me. He gave me a quick wink before turning and quickly riding off with the two adjutants closely behind.

We began our march again, working hard to make up for lost time. I knew now that it would be a long and tough road ahead. We boys from the small-town of Cucumber were about to get our first taste of battle.

❧

At around 4:00 in the afternoon on November 5, 1863, the last messenger arrived from First Lieutenant Henri` Dumont. Dumont and all of his men – who were the finest and best trained cavalry regiment in the Confederacy – were never heard from again.

CHAPTER 9

Droop Mountain

Droop Mountain (or as the locals called it, "the Droop") is located between Western Virginia and the Shenandoah Mountains and serves as a natural barrier between the two. From a military standpoint, "the Droop" offers a commanding view of both the Shenandoah Valley to the east and the Five Finger Mountains to the west.

And it was a grueling mountain to climb.

We arrived at the base of the mountain around midday. We rested an hour or so, and then we were ordered to traverse a small road, hardly noticeable, heading up the right side of the mountain. As we hiked further up, the terrain started getting steeper. I noticed large boulders, and little by way of trees and vegetation. One of the wagons started to overturn during the climb; however, Boone, Caleb, and I, along with a few other men nearby, quickly pushed it on one side and prevented the wagon from falling over.

We marched extra carefully from that point on.

We arrived at the summit around midnight under dark skies, and I remember feeling a cool breeze. As I rested, I overheard someone nearby say, "Why, would you look at the valley below." I glanced over and saw a group of soldiers walking along the edge of a large rock outcropping. I walked over to look down at the valley while Boone and Caleb worked to light a small campfire. The valley below appeared to be lit up with campfires from one end to the other. It was hard to distinguish the stars above from the fires below. It all seemed to blend together. As I scanned my eyes right, I saw a small trail of torches moving slowly down the road from where we just came. Like a glowing snake, the line appeared to be coming from town of Lewisburg, which lay on the very edge of the horizon.

The entire town of Lewisburg had been set on fire.

One of the men beside me muttered, "Jesus!" He looked down at me and said, "Boy, lookie down yonder! Below is the bloated belly of the beast. And it be hungry tonight!"

As the others began to spread out, I sat on that rock outcropping for most of that night, watching the lights below. With most of our provisions unpacked, Boone and Caleb immediately fell fast asleep. I could not sleep. Thoughts of my father, of Black Damp, of Jed kept racing through my brain. I wished I was back at the house with Pa, fishing with Boone and Caleb, or even back at school letting Ms. MacCulcah ramble on about some such or another. I finally drifted off sometime in the late, late night, but right before, I remembered to recite a prayer.

Lord, please watch over Boone, Caleb, and Captain Patton. And take care of Pa.

And God, if anyone is to die…. let it be me. But before you put me out of my misery let me PLEASE have my vengeance.

❧

Having fallen asleep on that rock, it wasn't too much later and still dark as coal when I was nudged awake by Caleb. He brought me some coffee and pointed to where he and Boone had set up camp. We wandered over to the small fire, making sure that we did not step on anyone sleeping on the ground. Both Boone and Caleb had also seen the Yankee torches that night.

I spoke first.

"Fellers, this is not your fight. You don't have to do this on my account. From the look of things, we're in for one hell of a fight."

"Shut up," replied Boone, clutching his coffee in his hand.

"Yeah…s…s-hut…up," Caleb repeated.

"Your Pa took us in when there was no one else," continued Boone, looking over at Caleb and smiling wistfully. "Your Pa fed us, kept us safe, put a roof over our heads, educated us, saved and baptized us. Hell…he was our Pa too!"

Despite everything, I couldn't help but to smile at my friends. "True enough," I said, "but I have nothing to live for. Aside from you two, they have taken away everything. Everything."

A long pause. "The three of us have e…e-ach other,'" finally whispered Caleb, fighting back his tears.

I smiled. He was right. The three of us have each other.

It was early morning when Sergeant Hatfield marched up and said that we needed to go over to a small clearing on the left side of the road. We were ordered to dig in at the tree line.

"Boys…I want a ditch line about three feet deep, running from end to end of that field," he said, pointing to the middle of the trees. "Reinforce the top of the ditch with logs, stones, or whatever you can find, and face it down the road. I do not…I repeat DO NOT… want any Yankees to overtake your position. If that happens, they will outflank us and then there'll be hell to pay. HEAR ME?"

All the soldiers nearby stood up and saluted. "YES SIR!"

We got to work.

We began to dig…and dig….and dig some more. Every two hours or so, a wagon would come by with water. We didn't even eat that day. There was no time. Others brought in stones, rocks, and brush to hide the ditch line. It concealed our position and helped provide shelter from the anticipated assault.

Around midday, Bill Ford came up to us and said, "You boys have been selected by the powers that be to hold the regimental colors." He looked away from us with his head down. Considering we were new, I thought that this was quite an honor. The three of us readily accepted. He looked around and said that because the line was not entirely straight, we should position ourselves along a small bump out in the middle.

We would stick out like a sore thumb.

At the time we felt such pride. After that, we attempted to dig that much deeper.

Little did we know.

We finished late in the afternoon and lay down, exhausted, filthy, and hungry. Most (including us) just slept where they dug. At around six that evening, a slight drizzle woke us up. As we stretched and yawned awake, coffee was being brewed and fires were being lit for the night.

That evening, we sat around our small fire. After some time, Jack Hinson "Old Jack" wandered over to us.

"You feller's ok?' he asked. "This being your first fight an all."

"We're fine," we replied in unison. Glancing at the flag, Old Jack asked in a whisper, "I hear tell that you boys are going to hold the regimental flag?"

I spoke up. "Yes sir, we are, and we will hold it most proudly!" Boone and Caleb nodded in agreement.

Looking around and then back to us, he whispered "Boys, some would consider that to be an honor. But they be dead. You understand that most all of the Yankee fire will be directed straight at you?"

We were stunned. We didn't even think about something like this. I swallowed, forcing myself to smile. Boone and I exchanged glances before he spoke. "Thank you sir, we'll be ready,' he said, calmly. He stood up and gently placed his arm around Old Jack's shoulder, politely turning him away. I watched as he whispered something in Old Jack's ear. Old Jack nodded and then, glancing over at Caleb, walked away.

In order to pass the time, the three of us took out our knives to play a game of Mumblety-Peg. Boone drew a circle in the dirt and scraped away loose stones, leaves, and sticks.

To see which one of us would go first, we took turns flipping our knives into the dirt. The knife that's in the ground the deepest and sturdiest goes first.

But just as we were starting to play, Old Jack wandered back into our little encampment. Glancing at Boone and then at me, he looked squarely at Caleb and said, "Caleb. You be ordered to be a spotter."

Caleb stood up with a look of disbelief. We could see his cheeks turning red under the campfire glow. He looked over at Boone and stuttered, "Booney...w...w-ould that be ok?"

Boone stood up and turned away from Caleb. Wiping his eyes with his shirtsleeve, he said in a strong voice, "Sure little brother. But be mindful. And do what Old Jack tells you to do."

With that, Caleb grabbed his rifle and gear and followed Old Jack up the hill behind the line.

Needless to say, at that point, we were in no mood to play Mumblety-Peg. A heavy fog settled in on top of the ole' Droop that night. We made sure that the regimental flag was secured and the line of fire was uncluttered before we lay down for the night. Only then did we try and get some rest.

Around midnight I heard Boone whisper over to me in the darkness. "You asleep?"

"Naw," I replied. "Can't sleep. How about you?"

"Yeh, me neither."

It was deadly silent except for an old barn owl cooing way off in the distance.

"Hear that?" Boone asked. "That's an omen, a sign of good luck." He was quiet for a moment.

"What do you think it means?"
I scoffed. I didn't believe in good luck anymore.
"Death," I whispered into the blackness.

CHAPTER 10

Unleash the Dogs of War

Our makeshift battlefield encompassed a small encampment of about 200 soldiers, located near the top of the tall, somewhat-rolling Droop Mountain. The top of the mountain, to our rear, provided excellent cover for both cannon and sharpshooter. Old Jack and Caleb were positioned there on the mountain's crest.

The remainder of the troops spread out on the other side of the mountain, which was far more level – the attack by the Yankees was predicted to be at that point. The woods, to the left of our battle line, sloped downward sharply, and at the end closest to ours, was a single dear trail. It would have been extremely difficult for any regiment in number to climb such a narrow path. The small dirt road used by us to get to this position sat to the right of our line, with 10 feet of woods directly beyond and then a straight drop downward to the valley below. In front of us lay a small clearing of about 100 yards, more or less, and beyond that, more dense forest.

Looking down from the top of The Droop, our line appeared to be similar to a frown, with Boone and I located in the middle.

This section stuck out the furthest.

Boone and I took turns trying to sleep that night. I would doze for about an hour, and then Boone would try to get some rest. The fog was so thick that I could stick out my rifle and not see the end of it. All was as quiet as a church mouse.

Early in the morning on that day – November 6, 1863 – a single voice rang out from the fog from the top of the mountain.

It was Caleb.

"THEY'RE H…H-ERE!"

Instantly, Boone and I jerked awake and jumped up. We kept our heads low and looked out upon the field in front. The fog seemed to have thickened even more. Nothing…we heard and saw nothing. I looked both right and left along our line and it seemed that all of the men stood frozen like us, searching….and waiting.

I heard a whisper off to my left, toward the road from our line. "Keep your heads down, and no talking!"

Silence.

Suddenly, I both heard and felt someone entering our trench from behind us. Boone and I both spun around. I grabbed my pistol and Boone his Bowie knife.

It was Caleb! Apparently, he was able to sneak away unde-tected, as all eyes were on the fog, scanning for the approaching enemy.

"Damnit, Caleb!" hissed Boone. "Get back to your position – NOW!"

"No way!" Caleb whispered back. "I want to be with
y…y-ou!"

"Caleb," I whispered, "where are they?"

Caleb looked at me, his eyes as large as saucers. "At the
edge of the tree line at the end of the f…f-ield!"

We stared straight ahead, but again I didn't see or hear
anything.

"Caleb," whispered Boone, "get behind me, and stay
behind me. You can load for us when we shoot. Load and
shoot, load and shoot…got it?"

"Aw Boone, I'm about as good with a rifle as you are!'
whined Caleb.

"Shut up!" whispered Boone, his voice sounded pained,
twisted in frustration.

"You s…s-hut up!" replied Caleb, a little louder.

From our line to the right of us a louder voice snapped,
"YOU BOTH SHUT UP!"

As time stretched out for what felt like forever, the fog
slowly, slowly began to lift. Caleb again was the first to spot
what lay ahead. As I stared out onto the field, I noticed the
sunlight begin to break through. A lone man appeared first,
sitting tall upon a white horse. He seemed to stare straight
at me.

Straight into my soul.

The man on the white horse began to slowly ride up and
down the opposite tree line, as if reconnoitering our position
from the woods to our right and the road to the left.

I could now see that one-third of the entire field in front, from end to end, contained Union soldiers.

Not one shot was yet fired. No one spoke from either side. We were staring down at least a thousand men, all well-equipped. I would have considered it one of the most stirring sights I'd ever seen, if not for facing certain death.

Suddenly, from our side came shouts of, "Hurrah… Hurrah!"

It was Captain Patton. He slowly rode up the line and put himself between us and the Yankees. As turned to face us, you could hear a pin drop.

"MEN, CONFEDERATES, BROTHERS OF OLD VIRGINIA!

LET THIS DAY BE OUR OWN!

LET THIS DAY BE THE ONE DAY IN WHICH WE CAN DEFEND OUR FREEDOMS!

OUR LIBERTY! OUR FAMILIES!! AND OUR HOMES!

THEY SAY THAT WE CAN NOT WIN THIS WAR!

THAT WE ARE NOT AN ARMY…. THAT WE ARE NOT A PEOPLE!

LET THIS DAY PROVE THEM WRONG!

LET THIS DAY AND ALL FUTURE DAYS BE OUR OWN!

LET THIS DAY BE FOR OLD VIRGINIA!"

With that he took out his sabre, turned around, and facing the Union lines, saluted. At first, nothing happened. Then a single command was issued from the Union side:

"FORWARD…"

It had begun.

CHAPTER 11

The Fight

As the Union troops advanced, Boone, Caleb, and I just stared, frozen in place in shock. *Oh my GOD, what have we gotten ourselves into?* My mind raced in a million directions at once.

I was the first to snap out of it, my thoughts finally beginning to focus and turning into revenge.

"Boone! Boone!" I said steadily. 'You and Caleb get down! The rifles should be fully loaded and ready. Pass me my mine."

Not taking my eyes off the oncoming enemy, I reached out for my rifle but came back empty handed. I turned to look at Boone, who was still staring straight ahead with glazed eyes. I slapped him on his shoulder and shoved Caleb, who was also still frozen in fear, down under cover.

"BOONE! NOW!" I snapped. He turned towards me, and I saw sheer panic and terror on his face.

I surprised myself and lowered my voice and said firmly, "Boone…Boone…it's time to get ready and hand me the rifle."

"Ahhh, okay, okay…sure," he stuttered. Just then, a nervous shot rang out from the other side, and the bullet flew right through the regiment flag.

That seemed to snap Boone out of it.

We both knelt down into a firing position, with Caleb peering out from behind us, trying to see. Boone shoved him down again and then turned – rifle in hand – and faced the enemy.

As they marched towards us, we waited. Caleb finally settled down and peered out from under the log we had placed in front of us. The command was sent through our lines: "Lock and load…..lock and load!"

"HOLD YOUR FIRE!" a voice rang out behind us. "HOLD YOUR FIRE!"

How these men could come at us knowing that any minute we would let loose both fury and hell was beyond me. So much bravery, and courage…on all sides.

The Yankees had now closed in about 40 yards out, and the order rang out from a bearded Union officer on foot to halt. They did so in unison; I did not see any Union soldier out of step. Meanwhile, the soldiers on our side began to laugh and jeer. Some even climbed over the breastworks to taunt them into firing early.

Not one did.

A Union officer who rode slightly ahead of the approaching troops yelled out, "MAKE READY."

"TAKE AIM," he barked.

The three of us crouched down behind the thick log and into our foxhole.

A pause. "FIRE!" he screamed.

We heard thuds begin to hit our log in front of us, and wisps of air pieced our ears as musket balls flew by.

Boone and I looked at one another. We popped up from behind the breastwork at the same time we heard the command from our side.

"FIRE!"

We didn't have time to aim. We just shot into the crowd before us. I remember that the smoke from the gunshot was so thick in the air that I could barely make out any soldier, friendly or not.

As we reloaded, a command barked out from the other side "FIX BAYONETS!"

I finished reloading, and as I lifted my rifle up to my shoulder, I noticed that about one quarter of the Yankee troops in front had fallen to the ground.

Not nearly enough to stop the advance.

I took aim at the closest Yankee soldier in front of me and fired. He screamed as blood shot out from his chest. The man fell to his knees as if to pray and looked at his chest. He tore at the front of his shirt in panic, trying to find the wound. Then he just tumbled over and remained still.

O God, what have I done? I thought. *Please forgive me!*

I looked over at Boone as if to apologize when the Yankee's front line charged.

I reached for my bayonet when an enemy soldier vaulted himself over our breastwork and log, knocking me backward into Caleb, who was crouched down trying to reload his rifle. I fumbled for my pistol when I heard a *whump!* and the soldier fell limp to the ground next to me. I looked, and saw that Boone had hit him on the back of his head and knocked him out.

Caleb and I rolled him over and out of our foxhole. Meanwhile, Boone grappled with another soldier, and before I could react, Caleb reached down and picked up the revolver that must have dropped from my pants. He fired it point blank into the Union soldier's side, the jolt sending the body halfway over the log.

He did not move again after that.

Just then, a bugle sounded from the field, and the Union troops began to retreat back across the field.

"HURRAH, BOYS, WE DID IT!" a Confederate soldier nearby exclaimed.

We stood up and stared at the slaughter around us, a sea of blue and grey all around. I took a deep breath. I looked over at Boone and noticed that his hands were shaking uncontrollably. Tears streamed down Caleb's cheeks.

I turned and faced the front, to the killing field before us. The Yankees, it appeared, had not really retreated at all. In the middle of the field, directly in front of us, they were bringing up a cannon. The monstrous beast lumbered out of the gunpowder smoke until its blackened funnel was positioned toward our lines.

It was pointed directly at us.

We just stared at this cannon, this…thing. I knew that there would be no escaping, ducking, or crawling away from its wrath. Like a breeze, we would be blown away. We quickly started to dig, to reinforce our position as best we could, but we knew that it would be to no benefit. Boone straightened the flag, pleading with Caleb to, "…leave, go, RUN!"

Caleb would have none of it.

So, in the end, we just sat there. When the Union troops were about 50 yards away, I watched as they loaded the cannon with both shot and shrapnel.

"Boone, Caleb….I love you both," I said softly.

As tears ran down Boone's cheeks, he tried to respond, but couldn't. Caleb stood up, wiping his shirtsleeve over his nose. He gave me a hug.

Once again, we heard a Union officer give the command.

"MAKE READY! FIX BAYONETS!"

"BATTERY READY!"

We crouched down as low as we could.

"FIRE!"

CHAPTER 12
Darkness

Darkness – a wet, cold mist – entered my body from all sides, enveloping me. It seemed to grow colder and colder the more it leached onto me, seeping into my bones. I awoke that afternoon, not with a gentle peacefulness, but with a gut-wrenching gasp of breath. I felt as if I was in a haze, clammy and wrapped in a chill, as if something was trying to suck my soul out from the recesses of my body. As I struggled, something lay atop me, holding my arms out from my body like a cross. Its breath overpowered my senses, hot and moist, like a woman hovering over her lover's mouth. The more I struggled, the more I felt its grip tighten. Suddenly, a noise rang out near enough to me that whatever was on top of me let out a slow hiss and slinked away.

As the grogginess began to disappear, I opened my eyes and saw that the sun was much lower in the horizon. I was bleeding from small cuts on my face, chest and arms as I slowly attempted to stand up.

That's when I noticed Boone. He was lying face up with eyes closed. Blood was covering his face. A large limb from our log had blown free and was protruding from his lower abdomen. Caleb lay face-down underneath him. The right part of his head had been shredded, with his right ear blown clean away. His left arm embraced his brother's chest.

I stood up, shakily clutching my rifle. I shook my head from side to side, trying to erase what I was seeing. I felt disoriented, and couldn't remember which side of the log I was on. I peered out onto the battlefield and saw Captain Patton still furiously fighting. Others, too, on both my right and left were still engaged in deadly combat.

Captain Patton stood in the middle of the meadow, about 50 yards away. The Yankees surrounded him in a large circle as he spun around, swinging the Rebel Flag to keep them at bay. Then soldiers surrounding him jeered and laughed, and I spotted his sabre lying broken at his feet on the ground.

"No, no, NO!" I yelled, more to myself than anyone else. Horrified, I quickly started to reload my rifle.

As I watched in horror, the Captain dropped the flag and fell to his knees in exhaustion. He knew that he had sealed his own fate.

"NO! NO!" I screamed. I looked around wildly. *Did anyone else see what was happening?* But in the midst of the confusion of battle, as the fighting ebbed and flowed, no one else saw the Captain and what was happening to him.

No one but me.

As I screamed, all eyes turned toward me, including the Captain's. As his eyes focused on mine, he slowly shook his head from side to side and mouthed one word:

GO.

Then the Captain smiled sadly and winked at me as the man in the white horse slowly approached him, pistol drawn. As he looked down from his horse, he spat on the side of the Captains face. And As Captain Patton turned toward his adversary, the officer fired.

The Captain's head shot back like someone had punched him. He fell backwards onto the ground and then lay still. Blood poured out from the single bullet hole in his head.

Again, I screamed, "NOOOOOOO!" Hurriedly I raised my rifle. In that chaotic moment, I thought that maybe I could kill that son of a bitch before his executioners would become my pursuers. I carefully took aim and fired…and then I witnessed the man on the white horse grab his cheek.

But before I could even react, however, I suddenly heard a voice behind me. "Finally, he's dead." I froze, instantly recognizing the voice. "I told you I would be back to settle the score," the voice said again, this time lower and with a hiss.

It was the dandy. Lawrence Perceval Rutherford III. Captain Patton's nephew.

"Go to hell," I snarled, staring him straight in the eyes.

"They're all dead. It's just you and me now, boy," he replied, slowly smiling a twisted smile. There didn't seem to be a single scratch on him. Hell, the fancy uniform that he wore wasn't even dirty. I looked back toward Captain Patton lying on the ground and started to seethe in anger. I just knew that Lawrence Perceval Rutherford III had hid during the battle. That the dandy (as Boone called him) was a coward.

At that moment, he leapt from what remained of the old log atop our battered breastwork. As he jumped, I caught glimpse of a knife in his right hand. I whirled to my left to avoid the knife, but his blade caught me along my left check, leaving about a three-inch cut. As I turned to face him, he tackled me and my head hit the top of our trench. I reeled in pain. Looking for a weapon, I spotted Boone's Bowie knife on the ground. I quickly lunged for it, grabbing it with my right hand. I rolled over just as Perceval jumped on top of me.

His eyes exposed a look of his surprise. He looked at the Bowie knife sticking in his chest.

He fell down. Dead.

I sat there in disbelief. I looked down at his body and his empty eyes just stared back. I had no choice. I had just killed the Captain's nephew. One of us. *Who was the traitor now?*

My gaze then turned to Boone and Caleb. My best friends. My only remaining family. A sorrow and sickness welled up inside of me. I turned away and retched violently for several minutes until I had nothing left, shaking uncontrollably.

I had to get my thoughts together. Our cavalry. First Lieutenant Henri` Dumont never showed up. There was never going to be any victory. I felt alone. There was really nothing here for me anymore.

Everyone had joined my father.

Looking around now it seemed that the majority of the fighting had subsided and only pockets of resistance remained. My pursuers were caught up in their own personal encounters.

I quickly picked up my satchel and grabbed what little provisions were lying around, stuffing them into the satchel with a small bag of gunpowder and shell. I then turned, knelt down and said the prayer that Captain Patton had said over Jed's grave.

Crushed and defeated, I picked up my rifle, turned, and walked away.

CHAPTER 13

Loneliness

As I walked away from my best friends, my senses started to come back. I overheard the moaning and cries of pain across the battlefield. Some of the soldiers cried for their wives, children, or mothers. Some made sounds that I could not make out. I attempted to help those that I passed by giving a drink of water or wrapping up a bloody leg or arm. One man had been shot in the chest, and as I knelt down to help, he asked me to pray for him. I held his head and said the Lord's Prayer with him.

Midway through, he died.

As the sun was setting, I reached the woods and the old deer trail. I looked back. For a moment, I saw nothing. But as the smoke lifted there in the middle of the field, in the middle of all this carnage, rode the man on the white horse. In what seemed like slow motion, he turned his head and stared right at me. I now recognized my old foe, my nemesis, the devil himself.

Black Damp McCabe.

That sight will be etched in my memory for all of eternity.

He was too far away to attempt another shot. It would be a bullet wasted. However, my vow remained intact. *One day I will kill that bastard.* Quickly, I entered the deer trail and followed the path downward. At times I had to scale down the mountain by jumping, as the terrain was unsteady and dangerous. I climbed over fallen trees and large rocks.

It was early night when I reached the bottom of the mountain. There, between the valley and the bottom of Droop Mountain, flowed a small creek. Under a pale moonlight, I quickly took off my clothes and washed and cleaned the cuts and scrapes on my body. I cut a small portion of cloth from the powder bag and attempted to clean the cut on my cheek.

The water seemed to renew me and I found new strength. Once dressed, I sat down and attempted to cut myself off a good portion of the hardtack from my satchel. However, both of my hands shook with such force that I couldn't steady myself. My stomach felt queasy, sick from what I had witnessed earlier. As I pulled out a half-eaten dried biscuit, I tried to shake my thoughts away from what just happened.

And so, I began to develop a plan. That I would somehow form a vigilante gang with some of the boys in Cucumber. We would then hunt down that rat scum of a Yankee Colonial who killed both my father and brothers.

It made no difference to me whether I lived or died. In fact, I'd prefer death because at least my spirit would then be with those I loved.

However, to carry out this plan I first must travel through, and over, the Five Finger Mountains.

✺

The Five Finger Mountains were appropriately named because at a distance, the range of mountains appear as five "knuckles on a hand." The middle "knuckle" stood the tallest, and in order to reach it, one must first travel over two smaller mountains. It was the middle that I anticipated to be the most difficult. Fortunately, the first "knuckle" was located about a half a day's journey west from where I sat.

I was anxious to get going. I knew that if I sat down any longer, I wouldn't want to get back up. Night had fallen, but I didn't care – I grabbed my satchel and rifle and followed the deer trail out of the woods, heading west. The Five Finger Mountain range is imposing, and easy to locate. The deer path ended down by a large field, and for several hours the travel was straightforward. I did not find any type of path or trail but none were really necessary. This portion of the land was fairly flat and cleared.

I saw no one. There also did not appear to be any houses, crops, or animals nearby. I could intermittently hear cannon and gun shot in the distance. Apparently, the battle for Droop Mountain was far from over.

I rested as I needed to, but never for very long. By early evening of the following day, I had reached the smallest mountain. It was an emaciated and desolate place. The air was putrid and smelled of rotted flesh. Here, nothing appeared to be growing.

It felt like the end of the world. A slow death.

As I started my ascent, the hill had about a 30-degree upward slope. It was a good thing the slope was not severe as

I had no rope. It was lightly forested with dead trees on this side so I was able to grab on to boulders, rocks, and trees to propel myself forward and upward.

As a heavy fog began to set in, a cold chill ran down my spine.

Soon dusk gave way to dark. As I stood at the crest of the mountain, I turned back towards the way I came, and along the far horizon above the fog I gazed at the Droop. I thought of Boone, Caleb, and all the others who had perished the day before. I quickly made a small fire, laid out my satchel for the night, and watched the waxing moon rise directly over Droop Mountain. I could see flashes of light over the horizon, but otherwise, I saw no other light, heard no other sound, and slept with a restless uneasiness.

My plan was to wake before sunrise and make my way toward the second knuckle; however, I must have been more tired than I thought for when my eyes opened, it was mid-morning with the sun shining bright in a cloudless sky. I made a cup of hot coffee and ate the last of some dried perch. While eating, I mapped out the way forward, from this mountain to the next. From where I was situated, I was also able to closely examine the third and tallest knuckle. It seemed that luck was on my side, as I spied a well-worn path, winding up the second hill to the very top. I assumed that this connected to the path I saw the day before that wound up the third knuckle. After finishing the remaining coffee in my cup, I put out the fire, repacked my pack, and began make my descent.

I was right. About mid-afternoon, I reached the top of the second mountain.

The second mountain stood just slightly taller than the first. It also appeared much more densely forested. While walking or climbing, I was barely able to make out the sun or blue sky above. I noticed that the passage would disappear behind large outcroppings only to reappear five or 10 feet ahead.

The route appeared to be well-worn, but I saw no footprints of any kind, man or animal. When making my way down the other side of this second mountain, portions of the path gave way to rock stairs, which seemed to be carved into the ground.

By late evening, as I reached the bottom of the second mountain, the wind began to pick up, and a corroded stench permeated the entire area.

I started to sense a malicious presence.

Let me clarify this by saying I saw nor heard nothing. I felt, however, that I was being…well…*observed.*

Something was out there. And it was watching me.

The trees and their branches were weathered and broken at the base of the third mountain. They appeared bowed and bent as if some terrible storm years past had violently twisted and turned them into spiraling, gnarled fingers.

The stench became almost unbearable.

However, I remained steadfast. I was going to climb to the top of this third mountain. This was the quickest way home – nothing was going to stop me.

After an uneventful night's rest, I gazed up at the peak, and started my climb up the third mountain.

CHAPTER 14

The Hole

The start of the third mountain proved much harder to travel. What was earlier (more or less) hiking over two hills, now I had to actually hold on to rock facings and cliffs. The chosen path seemed to have broken away in several places; at times, it was hard to locate foot holes and rock crevasses. Often, I had to shimmy over to the next ledge, where the path would once again appear.

As daylight began to fade, I started worrying about the topography on top of the mountain, wondering if there were a path on the other side. If so, how easy would the descent be? After what seemed like hours, I looked up and saw where the mountain crested. After a few more steps, I reached up and grabbed on to a large boulder and hoisted myself up and over. I had reached a small clearing. Breathing hard, I turned and caught the last speckle of sunlight disappearing from the horizon.

As I caught my breath, I looked around. The clearing was very small and as I tried to light a fire, a cold, howling, November wind prevented me. I was exhausted. Saving the remaining food in my pack and what little coffee I had, I gathered some wood and made a small shelter.

I fell right to sleep.

This time, my dreams were troublesome. Boone, Caleb, and my father came to me. Like Queequeg from Moby Dick, their arms motioned for me to join them in death... and I wanted to. I wanted to so badly. But as I rose up and walked over to them, they came into focus and had no faces. I screamed, and turned to run. As I ran away, in the far distance, an oversized eyeball began to roll towards me.

I woke up in a sweat, heart pounding violently. I lay there for the remainder of the night, staring at the stars.

When dawn first approached, having not slept after my frightening dream, I decided to get an early start to make my way to the other side of the mountain. From that side, I would be able to view my little town of Cucumber. By using this shortcut, I would be that much closer to home. There, I could regroup and gather additional supplies. My hope was to form a small band of resistance fighters to go after the man who killed my father and who shot my friends and compatriots.

I quickly washed, checked and cleaned my cuts. I picked up my rifle and pack and started off. The path continued into the woods and I only traveled for about 30 minutes when I came upon...it. I stopped dead in my tracks, dropped my pack to the ground. I shook my head from side to side, not believing what I was seeing in front of me.

I was face to face with a colossal hole in the ground.

Now…let me be clear. This was not a cave, nor a small hollow. This was a huge, HUGE canyon, so immense that the town of Cucumber could fit five times over, and not even begin to fill it up.

It appeared to be, well, *perfect.* So smooth on the sides that there was not a single stray rock or root sticking out. A perfect circle. It seemed almost as if the sun focused all its energy on the one point, carving out a flawless spot on the earth.

I stood there in disbelief for a moment before my knees buckled, and I sat down hard, staring dumbfound at the hole. I quickly looked around as if to see if anyone else saw what I saw, but was reminded that I was the only person around.

"What the hell is this?" I muttered out loud, to no one.

The path appeared to follow the perimeter of the pit. I began to walk around it, slowly, gazing at this malformity. I noticed that the trees and their branches dangled over the hole, as if peering down below.

What was peering back?

I picked up a small stone and leaned over the hole to drop it in. Within seconds, the darkness of the canyon enveloped it.

I did not hear it hit bottom.

This should never, ever have been here. *What made this… and how?* I had only walked around half of the hole when I came upon stairs chiseled into its side. The path seemed to stop here.

I sat down by the stairs and waited to see if any noise or sound came from below.

None did.

I threw several more stones, but still I heard no sound. And it was at this point that I decided to walk down the stairs into the canyon below.

Why? What made me do this?

Every day since that fateful day, I have asked myself that very question. Curiosity? I have no answer. It was the decision of a youthful boy who needed answers.

And it was a choice I made that I have regretted for the rest of my life.

At the time, I thought I would descend only to a point where I could not see the sky above. I needed some light, so I searched for several sticks along the edge of the path and for low-hanging moss or dry grass to use as tinder. Within minutes, I found what I needed. I tied these together with cut strips from the gun power bag that I had been carrying. I lit these with a spark of flint and within seconds, my torch was ablaze.

I rested my rifle up against a nearby tree, as it would only slow me down, and climbed down into the blackness below.

CHAPTER 15

August

With a start, Boone woke up. The pain in his stomach was excruciating. He rolled over on one side and discovered Caleb underneath him.

What…? Where…? `

For a moment, he didn't know where he was or what had happened. He tried to sit up, but the pain shot through his body and took his breath away.

"Caleb," he moaned. "Caleb…oh, what have I done?"

Boone reached down and felt a large stick protruding from his stomach. He tried to look down but the pain kept him from bending his head. He told me later that he thought Caleb was dead.

With both hands, he reached down and attempted to remove the stick. He could not. He was able to, however, stop any further bleeding by stuffing some of his front shirt around the wound.

"Caleb…Caleb…you alright?" Boone said, almost a whisper. His mouth was dry and he tried to swallow.

No answer.

He took a deep breath and pushed himself up some, turning to look at his younger brother. Blood had saturated the surrounding ground.

"Oh Caleb, Caleb…look what they done to you," Boone wailed, beginning to panic as he looked at his younger brother.

Just then, he heard a small voice whisper, "Will ya s…s-hut up! The Yankees are all around checking on all the dead b…b-odies!"

Boone had never before heard such a wonderful sound.

Sounding alarmed, Caleb whispered, "And what do you mean, 'What they have done to me?' Do I not look alright?"

Boone smiled and said nothing. *He was alive.* That's all that mattered.

Boone looked around, and what he saw shocked him.

Dead bodies…. everywhere.

Turning around, he saw a large crater embedded in the hillside. The cannonball had crashed through their fortifications and exploded into the mountain behind.

"Caleb, look to see if you can find Reece. We gotta get outta here….now!"

Boone carefully rolled over and picked up his rifle, and then used the butt of the gun to slowly stand. At this point, he was able to see his brother more clearly. Caleb was missing most of his right ear and had numerous large cuts on his face, neck, and hands. His uniform was soaked in blood.

"Good God, Caleb!" Boone gasped. "It looks like the right side of your face went through a meat grinder. You're sure you're alright?"

But Caleb did not answer. He stood up and stared at a dead body lying along the edge of the foxhole.

"Boone…Boone…I couldn't f…f-ind Reece but look…" his tiny voice said, trailing off.

Boone looked and saw the body of the young Lawrence Perceval Rutherford III. Boone's Bowie knife was sticking out of the boy's chest. "Boone…Reece ain't here," Caleb said in a whisper.

Just then, a voice from behind yelled, "Hands up you… you…er… men!"

Boone slowly raised his right arm. He could not raise his left or else he would fall flat on to his face.

"You heard me, grey boys. Both of you turn around real…." But before the soldier could finish, Boone whipped around to grab the Yankee's gun. He told me later that he would have gotten it, too, if he didn't have that stick poking out of his belly.

But the Yankee soldier anticipated the move, and quickly bending down, swooped his leg under Boone's, which brought him hard to the ground.

The soldier dropped a water bucket he was carrying and quickly sat on Boone's chest. With two fingers, he pressed on Boone's stomach wound. He hovered two inches above Boone's face and with a sneer, whispered, "Don't…. ever…. do…. that…. again."

"DIE B…B-UCKET BOY!" screeched Caleb as he leapt from atop the foxhole with his knife in hand.

With cat-like reflexes, the Yankee soldier grabbed Caleb as he leapt. He latched onto him by the front of his throat and slammed him down next to Boone.

He looked at Boone, then at Caleb, and back at Boone. With an amusing grin, the soldier said, "My, my, what have we here?" He stood, drawing his pistol and pointing it down at them both. "Get up. Both of you!" instructed the soldier. "I'm as serious as a dead man in a grave. You move and I shoot."

Without taking his eyes off of the two brothers, he said, "You, Sasquatch...grab the runt and help him up! Walk that way toward our line....real slow."

Boone did as he was told, taking a closer look at the Yankee soldier. The boy seemed to be no older than him. His hair was tucked up tight under his cap and he wore a Corporal's insignia on his uniform. The soldier picked up his bucket, keeping his gun pointed on Boone.

Boone turned and starting walking toward the Union line. Caleb followed. They were able to take in what remained of the battlefield, and for the Confederates, it was not a pretty sight. Slain soldiers lay everywhere. They walked past the cannon that shot at them and passed several more artillery pieces in formation along the tree line.

"We bivouacked further back in the trees. You Rebs never saw us coming," said the soldier with a smile.

"We saw ya coming a m...m-ile away Yank," hissed Caleb.

"You did not," he shot back.

Caleb hesitated for a moment. With his fists clenched, he looked down and mumbled, "Stanky Yankee."

Without missing a beat, the soldier replied, "Asstard."

"Pinchfart," yelled Caleb.

"Fartnocker!" snapped the soldier, this time with a slight grin.

"Biscuit b…b-utt," Caleb said, laughing in spite of himself.

The soldier immediately turned his head to look at his rear. "I do NOT have a…"

However, Caleb interrupted. "You come back like a GIRL."

The soldier paused and said nothing.

Boone rolled his eyes, grimaced and said, in spite of himself, "Both of you stop it, now!"

Caleb turned toward his older brother and noticed that he was wheezing and breathing heavy. The walk to the Union camp had taken the breath out of Boone, and his stomach wound had begun to ooze blood again. The soldier looked at Boone and back at Caleb, and pointed towards a group of men at the back of the line

"I got him, runt. Go over there with the rest of the prisoners. I'll take him to the doc and come back for you when I get him situated."

Caleb knew that it would be useless to try and run with hundreds of Union soldiers walking around, so he did as he was told.

The soldier led Boone to a large tent. Blood was everywhere. To the right of the tent sat a large tub filled with bloody boots. The floor of the tent was wood, and cots lay scattered both inside and behind the tent.

The soldier asked a scholarly-looking man with a white apron to take a look at his prisoner and then, leaving the two, walked back outside the tent. The man agreed and asked Boone to lie down on a large cot. As Boone did as he was told, the doctor said with a small grin, "I see you met August. That one's as tough as a boot."

"Yes, sir. If I didn't have this dang piece o' stick sticking out of my stomach, my brother and me coulda whooped him real good," said Boone with a wince.

The doctor laughed. "Son, let me tell you that many a man, both blue and grey, has tried to whoop up on ole' August. But he be the fastest, quickest pole cat this side of the Mississippi."

The doctor cut open Boone's shirt and began to poke and prod. During this time, August walked back in. The doctor turned to August and said, "Boil me some water and get me some clean linen." Looking back at Boone, he instructed, "Lay still whilst I clean the wound and sew you up. You're lucky! If that piece of wood had pieced your belly even a half-inch further, you would have bled out as quick as green grass goes through a goose."

August walked away and came back with the requested items after a few minutes. The doctor instructed August to hold Boone's shoulders so he wouldn't move. He then reached into his back pocket and took out a stick, wrapped up in leather binding. "Open your mouth, son, and bite down on this. This is gonna be a' might painful."

Boone's head began to swim and nausea crept up in his stomach.

"On the count of three, I'm gonna pull this out of your stomach. Don't move."

Boone felt dizzy, and the room began to spin. "Hold on…
hold on…." he muttered, "if something was to go wrong…
look out after my little brother, would you?"

August stared down at Boone, paused and then whispered
something to the doctor. Boone could barely make out what
he said but heard his name and something a "Major…"
somebody.

"One…two…" and before the Doctor counted to three,
he yanked out the wooden limb. Boone bit down hard on
the leather stick and grabbed each side of the table. His face
twisted in pain as he howled, "That wasn't no count of three!"

Then he passed out.

∽

August walked into a small, fenced-in enclosure where the
captured Confederates were being held. He told the guard to
open up the gate, and walked in to look for Caleb. The small
boy lay by himself under an old oak tree.

He had been crying, wet tears smudged across his dirty face.

As August walked up, he looked down at the boy. *Jesus,* he
thought, *can't hardly be older than 10.* Kneeling down, he saw
that Caleb was fast asleep. Putting his hand on his shoulder,
he gently shook him awake. "Hey boy, wake up…let's get the
doctor to look at you."

Caleb popped open one eye and looked up. "I heard you
a comin' a mile away."

Smiling, August replied, "Did ya, now?" He stood up and
gently helped Caleb to his feet. "Your brother seems to be
doing fine. He was sleeping when I left. The doc pulled the
stick from his stomach."

Caleb stood up tall. "He's my older b…b-rother. He can be a handful, but I try to take care of him most times."

August smiled again. "Know what you mean. I too have someone I take care of."

"Name's Caleb. What's yours?"

"August."

August escorted Caleb out of the enclosure and began to walk towards the medical tent. While they walked, he looked over at Caleb and asked, "Are you from around here?"

"Yeah. Me, Boone, and Reece grew up a little ways from here in a small town called Cucumber."

"Cucumber? What's sort of name is Cucumber?" scoffed August with a small laugh.

"Well, I don't really know how Cucumber got its name but it's about 15 miles from the Town of Beckleyville" replied Caleb, kicking at a stone as they made their way through the encampment.

For the second time that day, Caleb did not notice that August drew in a deep breath and hesitated. A moment passed before he spoke again. "Er…sorry. Who is Reece?" he asked.

"Reece…well, Reece is not my real brother, but he's like a brother to both Boone and me. You Yankees killed his Pa."

Another pause. "Er… Reece died too, um… in the battle yesterday?"

Caleb wiped his eyes with his shirtsleeve and said nothing.

They walked the rest of the way in silence.

Once they reached the medical tent, Caleb tentatively opened the flaps, unsure of what to expect inside. Peering in, he saw Boone sitting up on a small cot along the rear corner.

Squealing, Caleb sprinted to his brother's side. He knelt down and gently wiped Boone's hair from his eyes.

"Thank god you're okay."

"I'm fine, little brother. Just a' might sore is all. You need to get cleaned up and let the doc look at your ear and face."

"No way," countered Caleb, scowling.

"You can trust them, Caleb. They took real good care of me, especially the doc and August."

Looking up at August, Boone said with a small smile, "Thanks. Didn't know if I could have made it much longer."

The doctor wandered back over to the group, having seen Caleb come into the tent. He inspected the crusted blood on his face and his mangled ear. "Come sit down and let me take a look at ya," he instructed. After a few "I see's" and "hmmm's," he walked over to his medical bag. Reaching in, he brought out a bottle of cleanser and disinfectant. He gently began to clean around Caleb's ear.

"Doc," Caleb asked, "is it true that p…p-ee can be used for medicinal purposes, so to speak? I mean if one were to use the pee…er…urine as a form of a cleanser? Jed said that…"

"What? Sweet Jesus, you remind me of my own son. How old are you?" asked the doctor as he worked.

Caleb hesitated. "Um…. I'm 15, but people tell me I look a lot younger."

The doctor frowned and said nothing. After several minutes of digging and cleaning, the doctor helped Caleb up from his chair. As Caleb's face was turned, he snapped his finger beside the damaged ear.

Caleb showed no response.

The doctor moved to his other ear and once again snapped his finger. Caleb immediately turned his head toward the sound.

"Ahhh," muttered the doctor. He looked at Caleb and gave a small, reassuring smile. "Son...I think you lost some of your hearing in your right ear. Doesn't look too bad now that I have cleared the blood away."

Caleb just stared for a moment, then frowned. Turning his head toward Boone, who was still lying down, he said, "Can you believe this? The doctor told me I lost some of my hearing in my right ear."

Boone looked at Caleb and then down at the floor. He said nothing.

Just then a thin, bi-spectacled Union Officer stumbled in. He wore a wide-brimmed officer's Calvary hat (which appeared too big for his head) with riding gloves tucked into his belt. His pants were too short for his long legs and in his belt, he holstered two side-arm pistols. A large knife poked out of his boot.

He walked over to the doctor, glancing sideways at Boone and Caleb. He whispered softly to the physician. August joined them, and they spoke in hushed tones, glancing over to the two boys.

After a few minutes, the Union Officer turned to leave. He caught Boone's eye before whispering to August. "After they get patched up, bring them to me."

❧

"After what has happened and all, you boys are probably a might hungry," the doctor said a while later, walking back to where Boone and Caleb rested on their cots. He called for an orderly to go and bring back soup, bread, and two hot cups of coffee. "Both you fellers rest. Don't you worry none about Major Morgan. He's our supply officer. August is his son."

After filling their bellies with hot soup, bread and coffee, both boys fell fast asleep. Around midnight, Boone woke up with a kick to his boot. Opening his right eye first, he looked up at August. He was standing above him, staring down and sipping a cup of coffee.

"Can you stand?' August asked, matter-of-factly.

Boone opened his other eye, yawned, and replied that he could.

"Good. Get your brother up and follow me."

"Caleb….Caleb…get up!" whispered Boone, trying not to wake anyone else. Wounded soldiers lay on cots throughout the medical tent, some sleeping peacefully, others moaning in pain from their injuries or fighting off nightmares. Boone was surprised that he slept at all.

"What?" replied Caleb groggily. He sat up and rubbed his eyes.

"I said get up! We gotta go."

Caleb glanced up at August and yawned. "Oh, it's you." He stretched his arms over his head and lay back down.

August sighed, reached down, and flicked Caleb's ear with his finger. "Now, Jonny Reb! Get up!"

"Gawdam you…you Yankee rabble," muttered Caleb as he fumbled with his shoes and what was left of his socks.

"Both of you follow me – and keep quiet before you have the whole doggone Yankee army down around our heads," whispered August, shoving at Boone as they walked out of the tent together.

Opening the flaps, they were able to see just how much the Yankee army encompassed the field. There were at least 50 to 100 campfires burning throughout. Being on the edge of the battlefield, it was not difficult to make their way through the encampment.

It was clear that the Union Army was very structured. There were at least five-to-eight men sleeping openly around each campfire. Two-man tents were set up behind those sleeping. The rifles were stacked in triangular fashion, making them easily accessible. For every campfire Boone counted, there was a single guard patrolling, wandering in and outside of the perimeter.

As they moved through the field, they began to see fewer and fewer campfires, and the darkness of the night began to envelope them. Soon they arrived at a portable wooden cabin, tucked in by the edge of the forest. A small light was on inside and smoke was coming from a metal chimney.

August knocked on the wooden door and whispered, "Fa...I mean Major...the prisoners are here as requested."

A response came immediately. "Show them in."

As both boys entered the cabin, they were immediately struck by the interior. It was only one room. There were two cots on each side of the wall, with a small table in the middle. Four chairs rested against the other wall. Mats were placed beside both beds and a small vase of flowers was on the table. A rope ran the length of the room, attached by two hooks. A sheet lay neatly folded up on one of the chairs. By throwing the sheet over the rope, the one room became two. A bit of privacy in a not-so-private place.

Under a single candle, the Major sat at the table reviewing what appeared to be a private journal. The leather-bound register had his name inscribed on the outside and was titled:

My Odyssey of Study within the Appalachians
By Major Stanley Morgan

The Major quickly put a small towel over the book. "You boys... er, I mean men... been treated okay? Has August gotten you all something to eat and has the doc treated your wounds?" he asked, looking the boys up and down. He had no expression on his face. He gave away nothing. His hawkish noise held thick bi-spectacles.

Boone replied slowly, with suspicion. "Yes, sir. We've been treated mighty good. Thank you."

"You boys have a seat. August, get these boys a cup of coffee," said the Major, motioning to the chairs.

The Major and the two boys sized each other up as August hurriedly prepared coffee. No one said a word.

"How old are you, son?" spoke the Major at last, directing his gaze at Caleb.

"Err...I actually l...l-ook older than I am....I mean, I'm older than you th...th-ink....I mean I am 15-years-old...... sir," Caleb stammered, taken aback by the question.

The Major narrowed his eyes slightly and turned his gaze to Boone. "How about you...they call you Boone, that right?"

"Yes, sir,'" Boone replied, not flinching or breaking his stare. "That's what they call me."

The Major sat back in his chair. His gaze shifted from one boy to the other. After several minutes, the icy confrontation was broken by August, who brought over coffee for all three.

The Major sat down his drink without taking a sip. He sighed. "We've not been formally introduced. My name is Major Morgan. I have been assigned to General Averell 2nd Division Light Cavalry Corps. I am the...supply officer."

Pointing to August, he said, "This is Corporal August Morgan, my ... er ... son."

Both boys glanced at August then back to Major Morgan. "Why...er...this war has been hell for all.... and everyone," the Major continued. "I don't think ole' Abe or Jeff Davis even thought it would last this long."

Glancing again at August and then back at the Major, Boone narrowed his eyes. "We don't know who these people are. If were speaking the truth, sir, you and your army invaded our lands. You rape our women, burn our houses, and pretty much destroy everything."

August choked on his coffee, but neither Boone nor the Major flinched at the words. The Major stared at Boone for a long minute, and then lowered his gaze down and said with a sigh, "Son, we've lost good people from both sides."

Boone, in turn, looked at the ground. He closed his eyes for a moment before looking back up at the Major. He let out a long sigh. "What do you really want from us.... sir? You didn't call us here, in the middle of the night, to discuss the shortcomings of this war. You need something....and I think it be us."

The Major looked over at August, who was staring at both boys, and then back at Boone. "You're right. I do need you. And I'm willing to offer you a deal."

And with that, both boys together finally sat down.

The Major motioned to August and muttered, "There's a half-opened bottle under my cot. This is gonna be more difficult than I thought."

ᴏⱴᴏ

The Major became more relaxed when he started drinking, putting everyone else in the cabin at ease, as well. He explained that he was searching for his older brother and nephew. He had attempted to locate them and at one point hired a detective from the Pinkerton Agency to track them down, but with no success. The last letter he received from them was postmarked Beckleyville.

It seemed the war had brought forth a new opportunity to find them.

August finally spoke up. He explained that he spent the past week reconnoitering the area, disguised as a wounded rebel solder. However, a wandering stranger gathers little trust.

"You need to take the back roads in order to talk to the locals," replied Boone.

"And that's why we need you," August countered, leaning forward in his chair and looking Boone straight in the eyes.

For a minute, the room was silent. Boone was the first to speak. "I need to talk to my brother about this...alone, if you don't mind."

"Of course," replied the Major, smiling a narrow smile. "I trust that you all won't try to escape. Step outside and talk it over. I am prepared to offer both of you amnesty."

Boone and Caleb stepped outside into the cool November air under a soft moonlight.

Boone sighed, running his fingers through his hair. He looked at Caleb. "Now, hear me out. This here's a fine mess. If we leave with them, we could go back home and restart our lives. Why, I'll bet you a plug nickel that we could still stay at Mounds and…" he trailed off.

Caleb looked up at Boone with a fire in his eyes. "He's still alive…I know it…I'm sure of it," he said defiantly. "Remember when August knocked you down and slammed me to the ground? Right before, I looked over and saw the dandy lying there dead, with YOUR knife stuck in his chest. You didn't do that. And I know I didn't do that. It was Reece! I'm sure of it. And I'm also sure he thought we were dead."

Boone said nothing but immediately noticed Caleb's lack of stuttering. He was surprised, but decided not to say anything about it. He smiled at his little brother, and thought about all that had brought them here to this moment. After a minute or two, he responded. "Okay, here's what we're gonna do. Without letting them know our plan, we'll follow Reece's trail along the back roads through Cucumber to Beckleyville. See if we can find Reece. He has nowhere else to go but home."

Caleb nodded in agreement. Boone turned to go back into the cabin and Caleb followed.

Boone shut the door and turned to stare at Major Morgan and August. In a soft voice, he said, "Major... you got yourself a deal."

The Major smiled and stood up, looking at August and then back at the brothers. "Excellent! Get yourself some sleep. We leave at dawn."

They slept on the floor and at the first light of day, they left the cabin. Thunder played a solemn hymn across the lower valley.

If everyone involved in this adventure was aware of what was coming, none would have agreed to the journey.

Before leaving, the Major made sure that each rider had a week full of food, water, and fresh clothing in their packs. Caleb protested some after seeing the tattered clothes brought forth for them to wear – a mix of used blue and grey uniforms, stained with blood and dirt. While dressing, he kept muttering that an entire complete grey uniform would be more acceptable and he wouldn't blame either side for shooting us. "Now," he muttered in frustration, "we have two armies against us." He quieted down when each traveler was given their own horse.

Before the journey began, August walked up to Boone. He reached behind his back and presented Boone the Bowie knife that had been stuck in the dandy's chest. The blade had been wiped clean and the handle polished.

"When I captured you, I saw this sticking out of a dead rebel's chest. Father...I mean, Major Morgan, didn't want me to give you two any weapons. But this knife will help you defend yourself," he said, handing the knife over.

"Thanks," replied Boone, looking down at the oversized blade. Glancing over, he saw Caleb watching. He said nothing.

Major Morgan rode up and looked down at the group. "Mount up and move out…. and keep it quiet! Don't want to raise any suspicion." Turning to one of the patrolling guards, he said, "Inform the General that I'm reconnoitering like we discussed. I will be back in about a week."

Like a bloodhound on a strong scent, Boone took the lead, followed closely by Caleb. August rode in the middle, with his father bringing up the rear. Boone led the crew through the open field, where a day ago they were fighting for their lives. He spotted the small deer path on the left. Most of the bodies had been cleared off the field of battle, but the weaponry, dead horses, and supplies remained scattered all about.

As the group entered the deer path, Boone looked down and saw footprints leading down the mountain along the trail. He turned around and quietly whispered to Caleb. "We need to be on this trail like a tick." He pointed down to the tracks on the ground. Caleb smiled and began to whistle the "Bonnie Blue Flag" softly.

"Shut up!" hissed August, riding up right behind Caleb.

Caleb rolled his eyes. "You shut up."

In a louder voice, August snapped, "No…you shut up!"

"Both of you shut up…NOW!" barked Major Morgan from behind August. "For Christ's sake, can we not all ride in peace for just this one moment?" he grumbled, glaring at both August and Caleb.

Caleb quit his whistling…for the moment, at least.

CHAPTER 16

Down

As I took my first steps downward, I quickly noticed that the stairs appeared to be chiseled into the side of the hole. Both the sides and steps seemed to be made out of some type of dark granite. The middle portion of each stair appeared especially worn down, as if frequently used. The jagged walls displayed no markings. I was swallowed by complete darkness. *Curiosity killed the cat,* I thought to myself. This was too amazing, so unbelievable that I had to investigate.

As I descended further down, the stairs curved around the side of the hole, similar to a corkscrew. I noticed that the stairs were not evenly cut. Some stuck out from the wall by only a foot or two, and some stuck out of the wall by more than three feet. Most were damp, and slippery in spots. The vile stench I had smelled above seemed to permeate the air like a heavy perfume. There was no breeze and there was no noise.

Not a single sound.

I scrambled further down, down, and down. As I came upon larger steps, I would sometimes sit and rest for several minutes, then I would continue on.

I lost track of time. I looked up to see if I could see any remaining sunlight, but what had been mid-afternoon had vanished, replaced by nothing but black. Any remnant of sunlight had disappeared, and aside from the small torchlight, the hole was utterly devoid of light. Eventually, my eyes became accustomed to its solitary glow.

Then, all at once, I caught sight of a small glimmer.

There was light below!

I couldn't make out what type of light it was. I needed to climb down a little further to see. I slowed down some, cautious, unsure of what to expect next.

I finally made out the outline of a small fire emanating from the bottom of the cavern. The fire illuminated about a 10-to15-foot circle directly in front of it. In the middle of the circle stood an eight-foot smooth, wooden pole, perfectly constructed in shape and size.

I could see nothing else.

I hesitated and slowed down even more. About five feet from the bottom, I cautiously looked around. The small fire appeared to be about the size of a campfire, and it was surrounded by stones. There did not seem to be any wood in the fire.

The fire just came directly up from the ground.

There was nothing else.

No sound. No movement.

I swallowed, and stepped down onto the sand floor.

And it was at this point that something hit the side of my head with such force that I became knocked out.

CHAPTER 17

The Trek

Everyone kept to themselves the first morning. Caleb and Boone rode point, while August and the Major rode about 10 feet behind. By mid-afternoon, the company stopped beside a small creek to water the horses, resting under a large Weeping Willow tree. As August tied up his horse, he watched as both Boone and Caleb studied the side of the creek. Suddenly, Caleb let out a small squeal and pointed to some marks in the mud. Frowning, August walked over to where the brothers stood, examining a footprint in the mud. He still did not trust both boys.

"What's this?" he asked suspiciously, looking at Boone, then at Caleb.

"Aw its nothin," said Caleb, turning away. "We're just looking for some cr...cr-awfish that we can boil for supper."

"Ewwww...that's sickening. You're disgusting!" groaned August, wrinkling up his nose.

The boys wandered further upstream. Not wanting to set foot in the water, August yelled after them. "Father wants to know the quickest way to get to the town of Cucumber and Beckleyville from here!"

"Tell him that we need to take a shortcut, away from the main road, and ride through those mountains to the right. They are called the Five Finger Mountains. Once we get through them, we will be about a day's ride from Cucumber," yelled back Boone.

Grinning, Caleb turned and chimed in. "Along the main road you Yankees may own the day! But we Rebs own the side roads… and the night!"

August shook his head and turned back downstream. He picked his steps, carefully hopping to avoid stepping on any crawfish.

After several minutes of wading in the creek, Boone looked back to see if they were being watched. Not seeing the Major or August, he turned leaned in towards Caleb.

"Did you see those footprints in the mud? They were a light single track. That may be Reece!" he said with excitement.

"I saw 'em!" replied Caleb with a grin. "It looks like Reece was going home the quick way."

"And that would mean to climb over the Five Finger Mountains," replied Boone, swallowing hard as he looked up at the mountain range.

"Then that's where we'll lead them," Caleb replied, grabbing another crawfish.

Thirty minutes later, Caleb's pouch was filled with crawfish and they turned back and headed toward camp.

August was nowhere in sight when they arrived. They spied the Major loudly snoring under the willow tree. They lay the bag of crawfish by the fire, spotted August wandering back upstream, humming a song. It appeared that he had taken a bath.

As he approached, August wrinkled his nose. "Don't you Jonny Rebs take baths? I can smell you boys a mile away."

Neither brother responded. As August approached the campfire, Boone spoke up. "Did ya hear me earlier? We found a shortcut to Cucumber."

"I heard you the first time. I'll go tell father, but first, I'm going to water the horses."

"Come on, Caleb," Boone said, looking at the creek. "August's is right.... we need to take a bath before we eat."

The boys pulled off their shirts. Boone's stomach wound was still bandaged however it appeared that the swelling had gone down. Caleb's ear seemed to be healing up nicely. They were down to their skivvies when August returned with the horses.

"Whoa! No, no!" he shouted. "What are you doing? Not here...geez... go downstream and wash yourselves!"

"What?" replied Caleb.

"You have got to be kidding me!" said Boone incredulously. "If you haven't noticed, there aren't no bathtubs around."

"If your shy, and apparently you are, then turn around!" said Caleb with a grin.

And with that both boys, laughing, shimmied out of their drawers. August immediately turned around and stomped off.

Amused, the Major cleared his throat and said, "You fellers take it downstream. Believe me, your nakedness is nothing that any man or women wants to behold."

Both boys' faces turned red. Caleb mumbled something about "them goddamn Yankees." Boone just shook his head as they moved downstream to wash off.

The boys came back to camp 10 minutes later with wet hair and damp clothes. As August sat down to read a book, Caleb spoke. "Er, excuse me Corporal? May I lay your bed role down by the fire? I believe that this evening might be a bit chilly."

August, somewhat stunned by Caleb's kindness, replied, "Why...ah...yeah...that be okay, I guess."

Caleb took the bed role lying beside the willow and proceeded to lay and smooth it beside the campfire.

Boone and the Major served the group supper, and what a feast! The Major had prepared potatoes and bean soup with hard biscuits. Boone had cooked the crawfish over the fire, which they shared until the soup was hot enough to eat.

During supper, the Major asked about the people of Cucumber and Beckleyville. With mouths full, both boys told the Major about Mounds and about me. They purposely left out what happened at the barnyard dance, fearing that the two Yankees would know of or (worse yet) be cohorts of Black Damp McCabe. Boone steered the subject to the Five Finger Mountains. He explained that quickest way to Cucumber and Beckleyville was to traverse the imposing foothills.

The Major yawned. "I trust you boys. So tomorrow, just lead the way."

As evening turned into night, a waning moon approached the horizon. The group could hear distant cannon fire from beyond Droop Mountain and occasionally see flashes of light along the far-off ridges.

Everyone turned in rather early that night. Having bedded down the horses, August was the last to climb into his bed role. All was quiet for about 15 minutes until August let out a bloodcurdling scream. Several crawfish had snuck into his bedroll and nested at the bottom. Everyone instantly jerked up, with the Major fumbling for his pistol. Everyone except for Caleb, who pretended he was asleep…. with a sly smile on his face.

CHAPTER 18

The Pit

❧

Genesis 4, Verse 15-16: *And the Lord said unto him, Therefore whosoever slayeth Cain, vengeance shall be taken on him seven-fold. And the Lord set a mark upon Cain, least any finding him should kill him. And Cain went out from the presence of the Lord, and dwelt in the land of Nod, on the east of Eden.*

❧

I woke up with a start. My head felt like a lump of dried horse meat. The back felt swollen and bruised, and as I opened my eyes, I could see a pool of blood at my feet. I was standing, or at least, I *felt* like I was standing. I had no feeling in either of my legs. As my head cleared, I realized that my hands were tied behind me with what seemed like rough, handmade hemp. My wrists were bent forward, tied behind the pole and around my back.

How long have I been here?

I had no idea. I did know, or felt, that physically I was almost done for. With everything that had happened, and in my excitement, I hadn't eaten or drank any water for a very long time. The back of my neck throbbed unmercifully, and the cut on my cheek felt extremely sore and was bleeding again.

It was completely, utterly silent. I could only hear my gasping breath. I spent the next several minutes gulping down air and trying to get my bearings. Once I was calm enough to look up, I saw the small fire burning about eight to ten feet in front of me. To the left of the fire were the stairs that I climbed down. When I looked the other way, however, I caught sight of a small opening along the opposite end of the cavern. I had to squint my one good eye – the other being covered in blood – and stare at it for several seconds. I could barely make it out, but it was there – a doorway which blended into the darkness.

As my head began to clear further, it was then that I noticed them.

Red eyes. They were staring at me from beyond the fire's light.

They were all shape and sizes. Several blinked. But I heard neither a growl nor snarl. I looked back at the fire – it seemed to be getting smaller. It almost felt as if whatever was behind those eyes were watching and waiting.

It was as if they were waiting for the fire to go out.

Panic started to set in. I felt bile trying to come up my throat as I started breathing heavier, my eyes darting back and forth. I struggled with the rope around my wrists.

"WHO ARE YOU CALLED?" a voice commanded from inside my head.

"ARE YOU GERSHONITE? ESORIAN?"

I gave no answer, not knowing what to say.

"PERHAPS A LEBAOTHIN, OR A SHAALAB-BINIAN?"

I remained speechless. I pulled at the twine, feeling it rub my wrists raw. After several minutes of silence, I finally found the courage to speak up.

"W…w-ho are y…y-you?" I asked, my voice quivering. "W…w-here am I?"

For what seemed like an eternity, there was no response. Nothing but silence. And then…

"THE DEVIL'S WELL, THE GATEWAY…… TO NOD."

CHAPTER 19

Payback

The ragtag traveling group of soldiers rose early that cloudless morning. The sun was not yet wholly visible, as the Five Finger Mountains blocked the morning rise. The Major put on eggs and bacon for breakfast and August made the coffee. Boone and Caleb, somewhat sheepishly, saddled the horses and repacked the bedrolls.

"Good morning, Corporal. Why, how'd ya sleep last night? With a full belly of cooked up crawdads, I slept real good," snickered Caleb.

Boone and Major Morgan chuckled. August smiled but said nothing.

They proceeded on their way after all were fed and supplies packed. These odd collection of travelers rode single file, so they stayed on the remnants of the same trail. Boone rode first, followed by Caleb and August. The Major trailed behind the rest, lost in his own thoughts.

The Five Finger Mountains loomed ahead.

The group could still hear cannon and musket fire from time to time, as the fighting continued to rage. The Battle of Droop Mountain was far from over. As the four journeyed further west, however, the noise of the conflict faded more and more until they couldn't hear anything but the sounds of the forest.

Soon, however, even those sounds disappeared.

They stopped about mid-morning to water the horses, and August brought out a pair of binoculars from his saddlebag. He unraveled the strap.

"Caleb, are those The Five Finger Mountains straight ahead? How many miles do you think it is?" he said inquisitively. There was a slight hint of a devilish smile on his face.

"I don't know," Caleb replied, sounding somewhat annoyed.

"My eyesight isn't what it used to be, but it looks like our trail thins at the base of the mountain."

"Give it here," replied Caleb, grabbing the binoculars from August's hands.

The Major rode up as Caleb peered into both eye sights and adjusted the scopes.

Boone sat still, staring ahead at the mountain range as Caleb lowered the spectacles and handed them back to August. He turned and faced both the Corporal and Major.

"It looks to me that we'll reach the base by mid-afternoon," he said, scratching his head "Boone! Don't you think we will reach the base of the mountains by mid-afternoon?"

Boone turned around in his saddle and his mouth dropped open. Both August and the Major stood behind Caleb. August held a finger to his lips, motioning to Boone to not say a word. It took everything they had not to burst out laughing.

Boone stifled a chuckle and attempted to keep a straight face. Turning away from Caleb, he smothered his laugh with a cough and replied, "Yes siree, Caleb! That sounds about right!"

With an inquisitive look, Caleb muttered softly, "Well okay, let's go then." Turning to face August and the Major, he elaborately took off his hat and swept it down to a low bow. "I'll take the lead this time if that be alright with your majesties." He turned and then rode off past Boone.

Boone slowed down and let Caleb pass by him. He paused as both August and the Major rode up.

"You know he's gonna be a might pissed when he finds out, don't you?" said Boone, chuckling.

"Boone, let 'em find out on his own, please," replied August, laughing.

The Major shook his head but smiled a small smile. "I've already fought one battle this week. Don't want another," he said. "I'm staying out of it."

The rest of the afternoon, Boone and August rode behind the Major.

Although none would yet admit it, these individuals were quickly becoming bonded brothers. *Frater in armis.*

Brothers in arms.

CHAPTER 20

(Exodus 3 Verse 14........´ Thus shalt thou say unto the children of Israel, I AM hath sent me unto you.)

I was now panicking. Big time.

The Devil's Well?!

The fear of that name gave me renewed strength and energy. I struggled wildly with the rope that held me.

The bindings would still not budge.

Think...Think...THINK. I tried to slow my racing thoughts as I stared at the fire, which was now down half its size.

I tried to ignore the red eyes. I focused at where the edge of the fire met the enveloping darkness, and caught sight of a six- to eight-inch, single claw pull back from the fire's light.

"OH MY GOD!" I gasped, my heart pounding so hard it felt like it could explode out of my chest.

As I struggled to free myself from the bindings, I lost track of time. It seemed like hours passed. My thoughts drifted from my father to both Boone and Caleb. I thought about the carefree days we spent fishing, hunting, and playing Mumblety-Peg.

Mumblety-Peg.

Of course!

My knife, my Excalibur. *Old Timber.*

I wriggled my hand to slide into my back pocket and felt for the wooden handle. I grasped it and pulled at the handle of the knife as I stared at the fire.

It was now down to a single flame.

I needed more time!

"Who ARE you?" I demanded.

Silence.

Again mustering all the courage I had, I yelled into the darkness. "WHO ARE YOU?"

No answer, but the presence was still there. I couldn't see it, hear it...but I could feel it.

I had to move. And fast. Before the last flame died out completely.

CHAPTER 21
Caleb

The sky began to shed the day's light when the small troupe stopped at the base of the mountain. All agreed that they could make the top of the first small mountain before night fell. They urged the horses upward, following the trail. The horses almost seemed as if they knew the way and easily traversed the path. From there, the crew could turn around and view Droop Mountain far off on the horizon. They unsaddled the horses in what little light remained and started a small fire. August began to prepare the supper for the night.

"August, put some black coffee on," the Major said as he walked into the woods to relieve himself. "God, I have to piss so bad my back teeth are floatin."

Caleb seemed to be in an unusually good mood. As he was unrolling his bedroll, he said "What are you two Yanks going to prepare for supper? I am mighty hungry with all that guiding and tracking. Why, I think we should break out the biscuits and fry us some pork belly beans and gravy." He looked and Boone and winked.

Boone looked away. It was difficult for him to control his laughter. He had to admit, it was brilliant.

"Hey, skunk eyes," called August to Caleb. "We need water for the coffee. Finish with your bedroll and then look around and find a pond or creek."

Caleb raised his eyebrows in confusion, but shrugged it off. Softly whistling, he finished with the bedroll and grabbed several canteens and a small ember from the fire. He wandered slowly into the woods. A few minutes later, he found a small waterfall cascading down some rocks into a pool of water. As he bent down to lower the canteens into the pool, he caught sight of his reflection in the water.

Around both eyes were dark, black circles, making him look like he was wearing spectacles. His face looked like a raccoon.

As the Major walked back into camp, a loud scream came from the woods off to the right.

"YOU FART SNIFFING PIECE OF PIG P…P-OOP!" yelled Caleb as he stumbled his way back, loaded with the heavy canteens. He staggered into the small clearing, dropping several of them.

"Caleb!" scolded Boone, "Cut it out!"

"But Boone, look at what he did to me!' shrieked Caleb. Turning to August, he howled, "Why I oughta take you…."

"Serves you right!" interrupted August, clutching his sides as he laughed wildly. "Guess you'll think again before putting any more crawdads into someone's bedroll!"

And with that he walked over to the fire, grabbed a spoon, and helped himself to some of the boiling broth.

As the group sat around the fire enjoying some supper, Caleb remained silent, munching on his food and glaring at August. At one point August wagged his finger back and forth at Caleb with a grin, bragging. "If you nap with this dog, you'll wake up with fleas."

This just made Caleb more annoyed. He took of his hat and threw it down on the ground, and sighed a great big sigh.

"Face it, Caleb," Boone spoke up, his fourth biscuit in his mouth. "He got ya real good." Smiling, he turned to August and asked, "How'd ya do it?"

August waved his hand. "It was easy," he answered with a sly smile on his face. "I made sure he was asleep first, and then I grabbed charcoal from the fire and rubbed it around both eye pieces of the binocular."

Despite himself, Caleb couldn't help but smile. "Okay, okay, you got me back. That was real funny and all. Sorry about the crawdads. Friends?" He stuck out his hand with a devilish grin on his face

Taken aback, August looked over at Caleb and hesitantly replied, "Okay...friends," as he took his hand and shook it warily.

"Why, just to show you no hard feelings, me and Boone will clean the dishes," Caleb said. Glancing over at Boone, he winked and then turned back to August. "Maybe afterwards, you would be interested in a stimulating game of Mumblety-Peg?"

CHAPTER 22
Biding Time

I stared at the single flame of fire. This was the only thing keeping those things at bay. I could sense it.

I clumsily opened the knife behind my back, and slowly sawed at the bindings which bound my hands behind the post.

A distraction. I needed a distraction. I needed to keep talking to sidetrack whatever it was and (whatever *they* were?) beyond the fire.

"WHO ARE YOU?" I shouted once again, this time louder and with more strength in my voice.

Still no answer.

Nothing.

Where did the voice go? Did I imagine it?

"My name is Reece. I'm from the town of Cucumber."

I frantically sawed at the rope, as fast as I could. I felt the first binding give way. I caught it with my left hand so it wouldn't hit the floor.

One more cord to go.

I didn't know what to say, so I just began to babble. "I....
um.....I was in battle on Droop Mountain not too long ago."

Now, whatever was out there felt extremely close. I could
nearly smell vile, rotted breath upon my face. The red eyes on
the outskirts of the fire seemed to be swaying in a demonic
rhythm.

Eager. Ready. Waiting.

I needed a major distraction in order to bolt toward the
stairs. With one swift motion, I cut through the final binding
and screamed as loudly as I could, "WHO ARE YOU?"

Finally, the voice answered.

"I AM...NOT!"

I wrenched free from the pole and dove for the stairs just
as the fire went out.

CHAPTER 23

Mumblety-Peg

After supper Boone, Caleb, and August sat down by the fire. The Major rested on the other side, dozing on and off and scribbling in his journal. Caleb drew a large circle in the dirt and scraped away all the loose stones and rock to make the ground even and level so that the three boys could sit at the edge of the fire's light to play.

"I've… um… never played Mumblety-Peg," said August suspiciously, glancing down at the circle.

Boone turned to face August and slowly smiled. His face glowed in the firelight as he brought out the Bowie knife from behind his back.

"That's a bit creepy," said August, taking a step backwards.

"Not to worry," Caleb replied as he sat down by the circle. He patted at the ground reassuringly. "We'll teach you."

"Um…all I have is a small pocket knife," said August hesitantly.

Caleb smiled. "That's all I got too." He reached into his pocket and drew out a (rather large) wood handled-pocket knife.

August paused and then walked back toward his father. He headed over to where the horses were tethered and, reaching into his saddlebag, pulled out an enormous kitchen knife. Satisfied, he turned back around with a smile and sauntered to the edge of the circle and sat down.

Boone spoke first. "Okay. Here are the rules. Each one of us takes a turn flipping the point of the knife into the circle of dirt. The blade is down. You begin with your pointer finger and go through all five fingers. Then you start on your wrist, then elbow, and then your shoulder and nose. When you finish with one side of your body you travel back down your other side of your body until you finish with your other hand. The flip only counts when you can fit all five fingers under the blade. If you can, you get to immediately flip again."

"Can. I....um...practice a couple of times?" asked August, looking at his blade.

"Sure," said Caleb, smiling mischievously. "To show you we're good sports and all, we'll give you the first toss."

August took hold of the cooking knife and balanced the point of the blade on his left pointer finger. Carefully, he rocked back the knife and launched it forward.

Boone and Caleb forgot to explain that the launch needed to be downward, facing toward the ground.

The blade flew forward and across the circle and stuck into Caleb's leg.

"OWWWWW...you rotten son of a..." shrieked Caleb, grabbing ahold of his leg.

"Oh no! Sorry.... didn't mean to do that," August said, surprised. His face turned a deep red and he shoved his hands in his pockets.

Boone reached over to Caleb and drew out the blade. It wasn't embedded very deep.

"Aw, Caleb, quit your fussin'. It's mostly stuck in your coat," said Boone. Handing the knife back to August, he gave a lopsided grin and said, "You need to point your finger and the knife towards the ground and not towards the person across the circle."

'Okay.... sorry Caleb," said August, trying to stifle a laugh. "Really am."

Caleb just frowned and rubbed his leg.

"Okay, my turn," said Boone. Boone skillfully poised the tip of the Bowie knife on his right finger and flipped it to the ground. It stuck perfectly. Boone slid all five fingers under the blade and grinned. "My turn again."

He was able to reach his middle finger when the blade hit a small pebble and fell to the ground.

"I'm next," said Caleb. He furrowed his brow and stuck his tongue out sideways as he concentrated. He positioned the blade on his finger and flipped it down to the ground. "Ha, it stuck! My turn again!" he squealed excitedly.

"Wait, hold on a minute," August piped up, looking at Caleb and then at Boone. "Don't you have to get all five of your fingers underneath the blade for it to count?"

Caleb stopped, inches from pulling the knife from the dirt.

"He's right, Caleb. Check the toss to see if it counts," Boone said, raising his eyebrows and pointing at the knife.

Caleb frowned and tried to put all five fingers under the blade, but half of his pinky finger did not fit.

Caleb looked over to August with annoyance, grabbed the knife from the dirt, and sat back down with a "harrumph."

August grinned. "My turn," he said, carefully positioning the knife on his pointer finger.

"Careful....careful....careful," repeated Boone softly.

This time, August moved to fling the blade toward the ground, but at the last second, he flinched.

"Ouch!" he barked, pulling back his hand to inspect a small cut, which was starting to bleed. He looked up and saw that the knife had stuck in the dirt between Boone's legs, just inches from his crotch.

Boone let out a long sigh, his eyes wide in shock.

"Jesus, August, are ya really that bad? How are you Yankees ever gonna win this war?" muttered Caleb as he reached over and pulled the blade from the dirt and from between Boone's legs.

As the night progressed, August got better and better. The game ended when August, who was in second place behind Boone, tried to launch the knife into the dirt from his nose. It was a good toss; however, it cut the tip of his nose, small drops of blood dripping down his face. August frowned, wiped the blood from his nose, and stood up.

"This is a stupid game anyway," he said, putting the knife in his pocket. He stomped off to bed as Boone and Caleb looked at each other and laughed.

"It is kind of is a stupid game, isn't it?" said Caleb as they stood up and stretched, ready for sleep anyway.

Boone smiled and shrugged. *Stupid or not,* he thought, *sometimes the most ordinary of things can take your mind off losing a friend.*

CHAPTER 24

My Escape

As the last flame from the fire burned out, I dove for the stairs. I remembered from the climb down that I must stay close to the wall on my left. Frantically, I raced up the stairs, gripping the wall as I climbed. The – *things* – with the red eyes gave chase, stinging and clawing at my feet, trying to pull me back down. With gnashing fangs, their faces took on distorted, odd shapes. Although I didn't get a good look at them, I caught glimpse of grotesque, humanoid faces. The creatures tore into my skin, and I could feel the blood begin to trickle down my back and legs onto my feet.

I climbed…and climbed…and climbed. At one point, I slowed down enough to catch my breath, and several of the beasts caught up and jumped on my back, tearing into my shoulders and arms. I grabbed at them, flinging them off and into the blackness below. One jumped on top of my face and raked its claws over the top and back of my head. I screamed and instinctively grabbed it, bashing it against the wall.

It was at this point that I now sensed a third presence. Like a maestro, it was directing its orchestra to drag me back down.

Down into the Devil's Well. Down to the Master.

I looked up. There was no rescuing light. With blood in my eyes, I missed a step and rolled back and off the side. Fortunately, a three-foot precipice ran out of the wall two steps below, and I was able to grab the end to stop my fall. As if sensing my exhaustion, the creatures viciously pounced. I managed to kick my left leg up and over the step and pulled my body forward.

And still I climbed. I could see nothing but black, feeling my way upward, staying close to the cavern wall.

I was so tired, so very tired. An exhaustion like I'd never felt in my life began to crowd my thoughts and cramp my legs. When I attempted to pause or to catch my breath, I would be reminded by the creatures nipping at my heels.

After what seemed like hours, I saw a small glimmer of light. The beacon of Heaven!

At this point, I didn't know or care from where it came. If it was from a single star, the moon, or sunlight, I didn't care, as long as it broke the numbing blackness.

I envisioned that that single light was the eye of God.

I was mistaken.

CHAPTER 25

On Top of the World

The morning brought with it a cool November air. If a passerby were to catch sight of this group of travelers, they would have seen two young boys dressed in a miscellaneous assortment of Yankee blue and Confederate gray, a young Yankee soldier with bandages on his fingers and nose, and a tall Yankee officer bringing up the rear, oftentimes engrossed in a book or taking in the scenery.

Today, both the Yankee soldier and officer appeared to be somewhat apprehensive. For today they were to reach the small town of Cucumber and tomorrow, Beckleyville.

Boone rode in front this time, with Caleb trailing about 10 feet behind. August and the Major followed a little further back, keeping to themselves. The route led to the side of the middle of the Five Finger Mountain. They spied the small, single path leading upward. August took out his field glasses and noticed that the trail narrowed. There was no way a horse could follow.

"Boone, Caleb," he called, "we need to go off the path. Do you know another way up or around?"

Boone and Caleb looked at one another. Boone pointed to his left. "We could try and go around the left side through that hollow. We could avoid the climb, but it seems to be awfully wooded and thick with brambles and thorns."

August turned his horse and rode back to his father. The Major seemed to be absorbed in a wrinkled old map. "Father, what do you think? Should we go left and around the mountain to avoid the entire mountain range altogether? It would take another day or two."

"No, let's go through the depression and up the mountain. It will save us time and it doesn't seem to be too steep in most parts. We'll veer around the steep sections. Keep the horses in the middle. Through the binoculars, I was able to see that there may be a small clearing located about two-thirds up. We won't reach Cucumber or Beckleyville today, but it will be a hell of a view," he answered, looking up at the mountain.

August frowned, but turned his horse to ride up to the brothers. Both were stopped and waiting for instructions.

"Father said let's head left and up the depression in the middle,' August said, still with a bit of uncertainty in his voice.

"Gonna take a while to get through, but it looks like there may be a small clearing towards the top of the mountain," replied Boone, squinting as he tried to make out the distant peak of the mountain. Caleb shaded his eyes and looked, muttering his agreement. As August rode back towards his father, Boone whispered to Caleb, "That ole' deer trail stops over yonder. We could hurry the horses up the mountain and pick up Reece's trail from the other side. Since he left The Droop a day earlier, he may have already made the climb over the mountain. But August's right. There's no way these horses could crisscross that path."

"Sounds good to me," replied Caleb. Both boys followed orders and urged their horses left, forging a new trail.

It had been three days since the battle of The Droop. They arrived at the small clearing two-thirds of the way to the peak by early evening. Fittingly, they were on top of the middle finger of the Five Finger Mountain. As they cleared the brambles and thorns, the entire valley opened up before them. On the horizon, they spied a road and several houses, black smoke pouring from of the chimneys.

Boone and Caleb stared across the valley. Home seemed so very far away, but yet so close. So much had changed in such a short time – but thankfully, at this journey's end, they would still have each other. Boone sighed, and squeezed Caleb's shoulder briefly before turning away. Caleb rubbed his eyes, choking back a tear as he stared for a moment longer before getting to work.

By this time, everyone knew his responsibilities. Boone and Caleb were responsible for finding water and bringing back the canteens. Boone was skilled at building perfect cooking fires. He tended to wander around the campsite locating and gathering any dry wood, moss, or other flammable material to get a roaring fire started. Clearing out the campsite and removing stones, rocks, sticks, thorns or anything else lying about was Caleb's responsibility. August groomed and bedded down the horses. And all agreed that the

Major was an excellent cook. Whether it be preparing a supper or breakfast, he could make virtually anything taste good.

That night, the Major prepared a hearty French stew out of wild onions, water, and hardtack that he reheated. Each person was served two biscuits. After supper, the Major made hot black coffee.

At around eight o'clock that evening, the night had enveloped the mountain. A plethora of celestial stars peppered the night sky with the moon appearing over the distant horizon from whence they came.

And the mountain remained silent.

CHAPTER 26
The Reunion

I paused long enough just to catch my breath and looked up.

As I climbed closer and closer towards the light above, the attacks from the creatures seemed to happen less and less. The light was just bright enough for me to see beyond my reach; however, the presence of pure evil caught my breath and kept me climbing.

It felt so close. The same feeling I had at the bottom of this God-forsaken pit.

I rubbed my legs as I looked below. I saw something just beyond where I could barely see. It was intently staring at me. *Studying.*

I knew then that I had come face to face with...IT. The shadow demon that controlled the creatures.

It had a face that was incongruous and grotesque. Its eyes were large and oval. I couldn't see its body, but I could tell it was enormous. It revealed two bat-like wings disproportionately stuck out from its back. Its skin appeared to be blackish leather and the ears curved up its head, tapering into curved prongs. And what has haunted my every moment since that day was its smile, extreme and unnaturally wide, exposing rows of jagged, rotted teeth.

This creature from hell examined me and lifted a long, claw-like finger to its mouth.

"SHHHHHH" it voiced, smiling at me as a chill ran up my body.

I hesitated for only a moment before I let out a scream and raced up the remaining stairs as fast as my tired legs would allow. I imagined it trailing me only inches from my back, ready to drag me down and sink its fowl, decayed teeth deep into my neck.

It was so near that I could smell its breath. Like a lover's pant gently caressing, only this time, it would be the kiss of death. I bolted with all the strength I could muster. Looking up, I saw that I was very near the top.

So close to freedom.

For a second, something grabbed at my feet as I reached the top. I kicked and squirmed out of its grip, climbing out of the hole and rolling several feet into the woods.

There was no time to rest. There was no time to think.
I had one thought.
RUN.

The moonlight washed upon me and all of my surroundings. As I jumped up, I felt my legs give way to exhaustion, and I fell back down. Grabbing a nearby tree, I attempted to stand up again. I glanced behind me toward the hole.

Its head started to appear.

"AHHHHHH!" I yelled, terror winning the war against exhaustion. I turned and started running through the woods and down a small hill.

There was blood everywhere. My knees were crusted in blood where I had skinned and cut them on the stone stairway. I could not see out of one eye, and I could feel that I was missing most of the back of my shirt. I knew that I was weak. I hadn't eaten nor drank anything but some sips of water for several days at least.

A twig snapped to my right, which startled me. I didn't think that the creature or any of its legions would have reached the woods yet. As I ran, I stumbled through thickets of thorns and bramble, which tore and stung at my bloodied and raw legs.

As I looked ahead, I thought I saw a small light, just a flicker. It would disappear, only to reappear again.

God, let me make it. Please Lord…please, I begged out loud as I ran.

I started to recite a prayer that my father taught me when I was small. *Rescue me, Oh my God, from the hand of the wicked….*

Just a little further.

The light was beginning to come into form. I could see a small clearing with several people sitting around a fire. It was so very close now. I was almost within its grasp. The smell hit me like a sack of dirt. Putrid. Rotting. The smell of the dead.

I dove for the light and the clearing.

Four things happened at the very same time that night. First, as I dove into the clearing, I fainted into August's arms.

In doing, so his hat fell off, revealing long, black hair which was tucked up into the cap.

Secondly, my sudden appearance surprised the Major so much that he immediately jumped up, pulled his revolver, and aimed it at me.

Third, having seen the Major jump up, Boone and Caleb jumped up as well, drawing their knives and pointing them at the Major.

Boone gasped, then yelled, "Stop! It's REECE!"

And Caleb. "August's a GIRL!"

And lastly, a tall, broad-shouldered black man entered the camp from the east, holding up his hands. He did not speak a single word.

ఎం

But what I alone witnessed that night moments before collapsing into August's arms was that about 50 yards up on a small knoll silhouetted by the moon, sat the thing, the smiley creature, the demon or the devil himself...watching.

And waiting.

CHAPTER 27

Jupiter Moss

The broad-shouldered black man was named Jupiter Moss, and he was an escaped slave. Years later, he and I searched archives, historical records, and slaver manifests to piece together his ancestry. Until his passing years later, he became a father, brother, and best friend. Moss was kind, gentle, extremely intelligent, and one of the greatest men I ever knew, aside from my father.

He also had been a mute for over 25 years.

As best as he and I could tell, Jupiter Moss (I would always just call him Moss) was born in Jamaica in or around 1831. His parents were also slaves, all three under the ownership of Sir Thomas Thistlewood.

Now life often plays cruel jokes and Moss lived one the cruelest. Sir Thomas Thistlewood was perhaps the harshest slave owner of the 19th Century. A British citizen, Thistlewood claimed to have graduated from Ackworth College in

West Yorkshire with a medical license, but in reality, he was "self-educated."

And he often practiced medicine on his own slaves.

Moss told me that he didn't remember his father, but that his mother told him one week after he was born, Thistlewood attempted to force himself upon her while she was working in one of the farm's old barns. Moss's father, enraged, grabbed a nearby machete hanging up on the wall and started to slash and stab at his owner. To his surprise, however, the machete was not sharp, worn down after years of use. Thistlewood suffered only minor injuries. For Moss's father's actions, this cruelest of men gagged and flogged him for six hours. Thistlewood then took him, rubbed him with molasses, and exposed him naked to the flies and mosquitoes all night.

Without a fire, Moss's father did not survive the night.

Several months later, Sir Thomas Thistlewood sold both Moss and his mother to one Madame Delphine LaLaurie out of New Orleans, one of the cities wealthiest women.

But being the wealthiest does not equate to morality and goodness.

Moss and his mother worked the fields all day for six days in a typical week. The seventh day was a day of rest, minding clothes and generally preparing for the next week. It was around the time Moss was first clothed (about six or seven years of age) that he was taken from the field and brought into the basement of the estate. In front of Moss, the Madame brought forth his mother and had her strapped down onto a large wooden table. She ripped off her clothes and forced her mouth open while other slaves boiled hot sea water. They slowly poured the boiled water down his mother's mouth until she drowned.

All for serving from the wrong side of the dinner table.

Although she struggled at first, exhaustion overwhelmed her and she eventually just gave up. Just before she succumbed to the torture, she turned her head toward Moss and a single tear rolled down her face.

Madame LaLaurie forced Moss to watch this terrifying spectacle, from start to finish. It was at that moment, shaking in fear and horror, that this little boy became a mute. His mind could not overcome what he had just witnessed.

Afterwards, Moss once again was put out into the fields to work, lift, and plow. From then on, he made it a point to work alone, although others often attempted to come to his aid. When one corner of the field was being picked or plowed, he would work the other side. Where the slaves would gather to eat, he would take his food and go elsewhere. The overseers, who were often also slaves, left him alone. He always worked his share and never gave them any cause for alarm.

When Moss became a man of 32, he was then sold for a substantial sum of money to a wealthy land owner in Virginia named John Armfield.

His plantation was called Antebellum.

CHAPTER 28

John Armfield

Before the reunion… three months earlier…

"Steal away…. steal away….steal away to Jesus. Steal away…. steal away….steal away home. Ain't got long to stay here.

"My Lord, he calls me… he calls me by the Thunder…. the Trumpet sounds within my soul…I ain't got long to stay here."

It was a clear and sunny Sunday near Lynchburg, Virginia, and Jupiter Moss was sitting in the back row of a small church. For Moss, Sundays always felt like cool rain on a hot summer day. The master, John Armfield, insisted that all of his slaves attend his church every Sunday. Sundays, according to the Lord and John Armfield, remained a day of rest.

That day, Moss did not sing nor hum the gospel, but rather closed his eyes and let the words and music take him to a better place. *Heaven,* he thought as tears rolled down his cheeks.

Moss looked around when the song ended and, not wanting anyone to see him crying, quickly sat down. He wiped away the last few tears with the back of his sleeve as he tried to follow the day's sermon. The master did not allow any of the slaves the privilege of learning how to read or write. It was extremely difficult for Moss to interpret what his owner preached. He did not know what many of the words meant, nor did he understand any of the parables. He would try as best he could, but today, Moss felt overwhelmed with frustration.

"According to Ecclesiastes, Chapter 3…to everything there is a season, and a time to every purpose under the heaven," the master preached from the pulpit. Moss understood this. That part made sense. The master went on, "…A time to get, and a time to lose; a time to keep, and a time to cast away."

But this, he did not understand. A time to lose and a time to cast away? Cast away what? Himself? If so, where would he go?

As he sat there, he had far more questions than answers. He dared not reach out to anyone. That always meant trouble. And trouble meant lashings. And lashings meant pain, suffering, and loss.

Moss looked around to see if anyone else was having difficulty following. No one appeared as lost has he was. Similar to a frightened animal, Moss gazed straight ahead with his shoulders slumped down. He accidentally locked eyes with his master momentarily; he instantly looked away and stared at the ground. Not daring to look up again, he sat very still and listened until the sermon was over.

As church ended, everyone started to leave but Moss. He hung back somewhat, and was last in line to step outside. That's how no one saw as he slowly turned, walked back into the church and up to the podium, and took the master's copy of the illustrated Bible. For, you see, pictures tell a thousand words, and Jupiter Moss just wanted to know better the Word of God.

Moss exited the church through the rear door so no one would spot him and headed towards a large Sycamore tree in a field that they had recently cleared and plowed. Moss just wanted to try and understand more of his master's preaching. He would return the Bible that afternoon. No one would even know it was missing, and everything would be fine.

Or so he thought.

As he thumbed through the Book, he saw sketches of men and women. Much like himself! He saw a sketch of Moses and of an Egyptian man whipping a Jewish slave. He turned more pages, becoming more and more captivated.

What Moss didn't realize, however, was that his master John Armfield and his two slavers, Mingo and Quash, were beginning to look for him. And an hour later, they found him under the tree, totally engrossed in the good Lord's book.

John Armfield peered down from his horse at Moss, and as Mingo and Quash ran up beside him, he slowly dismounted. Moss jumped up quickly, panicked and unsure of what to do. He immediately handed the Bible back to his master and like a browbeaten cur, he lowered his eyes.

Shaking his head slowly, John Armfield spoke. "Take him to the barn. Let no one see you, or I'll whip you both like I'm gonna whip him." He climbed back on his horse and rode off.

The two overseers tied Moss's hands behind his back and pushed him forward so hard that he fell. As he struggled to get up, the men kicked him again, hard. They roughly forced him to his feet and escorted him to a large tobacco barn located by the main house.

John Armfield waited inside, a worn leather lash in hand.

Frowning, he sighed. "Jupiter Moss, I've been good to you. I have fed and clothed you. I have provided a shelter and warm fire for you. I even tried to get you some religion. And this is the thanks I get? Quash. Mingo. Untie his hands, get his shirt off and tie him to the whippin' post."

They did as they were told. As they tied his hands, Quash leaned in close to Moss's right ear and whispered, "You about as dumb as a Negra could be, boy. Any dumber and you'd be that there fence post."

Moss just stared ahead. As his shirt was torn off of him, the two slavers jumped back, surprised. Moss's back was riddled with lash and burn marks from his previous owners.

And with that, John Armfield, a husband of a loving wife, a father of three children, owner of 45 slaves, seven horses and a mule, beat the ever-loving breath out of Jupiter Moss.

CHAPTER 29

The Escape of Jupiter Moss

Moss woke up the next day lying face down in a bed of straw. He had thrown up during the night and was laying in his own pool of vomit. He did not have enough strength to lift a finger. His master, by the grace of God, saw Moss as more of an investment than a human being. An investment that makes money.

Some of the female workers tended to Moss's wounds and slowly he recovered. Within a week, he started walking and performing minor labor around the house and fields, keeping to himself. He continued to eat his lunch under that old Sycamore tree alone. Anytime the master or his two slavers came near, Moss would turn the other way and make himself busy, tending to whatever was in the opposite direction of whence they came. Occasionally, Moss would glance over in the direction of the overseers and several times caught them staring right back at him.

All this time, Moss remained obedient and cordial.

One very stormy and rainy night about two months after his beating, Jupiter Moss got up from his bed of hay and, as quiet as a church mouse, stole an 11-inch T Handle Hay Hook hanging on the side of the barn door. He then snuck into the main house through a side kitchen window and quietly crept upstairs to where the master slept. He knew that John Armfield slept away from his wife on most nights – his wickedness knowing no limits, he would often be found forcing himself upon one of his several slave women.

As Moss entered the master's bedroom, he saw that the female slave that evening was the one who tended his wounds. And she was not asleep. Moss's luck had turned.

As he approached the bed, he heard the master snoring. Surprised, the slave girl muffled a gasp with her hand. Her eyes were wide open in terror has she caught sight of the grotesque instrument gripped in his hand. Moss gently motioned for her to get up out of the bed and leave the room. His gaze followed her as she quietly closed the door and took off down the hall.

It was that night Jupiter Moss became a slave no more.

Moss had planned his escape with as much preparation as a spider crafting its web. Every time he ate his lunch under that old Sycamore tree, he would take a third of his food and put it in an old cigar box that the master had thrown out and hide it in a hollowed-out hole lying under a rotted root. Moss was not only able to store the extra food, but he was also able to store a few articles of clothes, a knife, and extra shoes.

He had waited for the perfect night. The rain would wash away all of his tracks, the thunder would drown out any and all noise, and the lightning would periodically light his way northwest.

It was around two in the morning that Moss was able to gather his meager possessions and start out. He told me later that he knew that his captors would think that he would go north or east toward the coast, as all who wanted to escape the south would typically do. But instead (which was brilliant), Moss traveled west.

As he gathered his supplies, he crossed over the plowed fields and groomed gardens of Antebellum, initially traveling east. Every now and then he would drop a small piece of cloth he had ripped from a spare shirt. At around four in the morning, he crossed a small creek. He walked about 100 yards past the creek and then reversed course, making his way back across the creek from whence he came, carefully stepping back in his footprints. Just an hour before daylight, he paused along the edge of the woods long enough to see and hear all the commotion from the main house. He watched as people ran about, wailing and screaming. Neighbors came sprinting in from all directions. The overseers Quash and Mingo, guided by the owners of the adjoining plantations, led four coon dogs over to the Sycamore tree to get a whiff of Moss's scent and off they went.

East.

Moss ran like the devil west, heart pounding in his chest. He was as scared as hell because he knew that not only would they hang him, but they would unmercifully torture the life out of him first.

After 15 minutes or so, he slowed down his running to a more methodical pace, making sure he stayed in the woods.

It had stopped raining earlier and a damp mist permeated the air. Every so often, he would slip or stumble, but would immediately get back up, not letting anything stop his progress west. It was like that for several days – running by night and sleeping during the day. Hearing no howl of hound nor voice in the woods by the fourth day Jupiter Moss finally felt for the first time in his life that he was free. Free.

FREE.

And to him it was a spiritual reawakening.

He rested for a bit before proceeding northwest at a slow jog following a wide river. He found a small cave under a fading sunlight. Bathing in the glory of freedom, he entered the cave with a full moon behind his back. There was a large spider's web blocking the entrance, so he belly-crawled in and nestled his way to the rear.

And as it turned out, that spider's web saved his life.

Premonition, a bad dream, or something else woke him up at around midnight. His eyes jerked open, and he saw a glimmer of a small torchlight glowing around the entrance of the cave.

Before he could react, Moss saw a gloved hand reach into the cave in the glimmering torchlight. He held his breath. For a moment, his life flashed before him. However, the holder of the torch saw the undisturbed spider's web and apparently decided that, for the moment, the cave was unoccupied.

The light glimmered and then altogether faded away.

It wasn't until dawn that next morning when Moss finally inched his way out of the cave. Scared and tired, he decided to travel more west than north.

Towards the distant mountains he saw on the horizon, and toward us.

◦◦

Moss traveled at night, mostly keeping to the woods. He rested and hunted during the day. He fed on small fish or crawdads caught in the streams. Occasionally, he would attempt to catch small game in the woods, but that took too long. He learned to be always on the move. For weeks, Moss made his way deeper into the woods, toward the Five Finger Mountains and our joyful band of misfits.

It was around the third week that the nights started to get colder. Moss began to hear a low rumble in the distance, followed by flashes of light far off on the horizon. It was the "killing fields." Rumors on the plantation told him that he would be shot on sight by Southern troops – and Northern troops were no better. They would stick a rifle in his hand with little to no training and send him off to die. *No way, no how,* thought Moss.

However, it was the rumble in his stomach on that cold fall night that brought him to our camp.

It was a full moon that evening when he stopped to rest. He sat, leaning his back against the trunk of a sturdy tree, rubbing his eyes with his hands. As he lifted his head, he suddenly, spotted – further up in the woods – a small flicker of light. Ever so cautiously, he crept forward. As he peeled away the branches, he spied a group of people talking around a small campfire. There were two Yankee soldiers and other two solders dressed in mismatching uniforms. One appeared to be of a small boy. Several tin plates full of biscuits and meat rested around the fire. As he smelled fresh brewed coffee, his stomach let out a deep, roaring growl. The two Confederate soldiers and one of the Yankee soldiers seemed to be just young boys, while the older Yankee soldier appeared more of a doddering old man. That night he sat for several hours in the bushes just outside the fire's light – watching and calculating if any could possibly be a threat, not only to his life but also his new found freedom.

Hunger pains ripped through his stomach, stripped away his reasoning, he couldn't think about anything but those biscuits in front of him. So close.

And then he remembered an old Bible verse.

Show trustworthy with the little, and God will trust you with more.

Moss slowly stepped forward, both hands held high, into the small clearing.

CHAPTER 30

Loved Up

As I drifted in and out of a weary sleep the following day, the only thing I remember seeing is August's face. She would sit beside me and hold my hand, ever-so-softly blowing on it from time to time to get my fingers warm. I learned later that sometimes Boone, Caleb, or the Major would join her, staring at me in disbelief.

I don't remember much more than that from that first day. It wasn't until the afternoon of the following day, when I was sure that I felt soft lips on my cheek and a single tear drop upon my chin that I began to regain full consciousness. (Years later, August told me it was love's first dream.) I slowly opened one eye, and then the other, and I caught sight of her fully for the first time.

"Ohh! Um...hello," August said, caught off-guard. A blush crept up her neck and into her cheeks, turning them a deep red.

I said nothing. I couldn't think straight. In her presence, although every muscle in my body ached, my heart trembled like a frightened dove.

She was beautiful.

"Who… who are you?" I asked softly, finally able to speak.

She gently let my hand go and set it down beside me. "My name is August. My father and I…ah… sort of…. um…. captured your companions. We were in the process of traveling to Beckleyville to get some supplies and search for my father's uncle and cousin."

"He… didn't… pee on me? Caleb, I mean," I askes softly, trying my best to smile.

She laughed and then said, "No…but he wanted too. Boone, my father and I convinced him otherwise. What's with that?"

She was dressed in a Yankee uniform. Her black hair, uncombed, was falling down both shoulders and her eyes, sparkling with life, were emerald green. She had a small cut on her nose which she kept trying to hide as she talked.

"Oh," I replied, too weak to say much else. My head was spinning, trying to comprehend what she just said. Boone and Caleb…alive? Captured by the Union army, heading to Beck-leyville? It was then that I looked down and noticed that all my scratches, cuts, and claw marks had been cleaned and dressed, and my clothes had been changed. My mind raced to catch up.

"Boone and Caleb…. they're okay?' I mumbled, catching myself drifting away again.

It was too much, *too much,* for my mind to take. I needed to rest.

154

"Yes, they're fine," she replied softly. "They went to get some fresh water and some small game for supper. Father... er... the Major said we can continue on tomorrow morning if you feel up to it. That gives you time to rest and to heal up. We can put you on my horse."

I looked at her for a moment more before my body gave up. I didn't want to close my eyes, but the exhaustion won and I fell back into the welcoming arms of sleep.

The next time I opened my eyes, there sat Boone and Caleb.

Boone and Caleb!

I could see the Major sitting directly behind them, his Union uniform drawing my eyes immediately. Moss sat by the small fire, roasting a rabbit and cutting up some carrots. They both stared at me with a fierce intensity mixed with curiosity.

Noticing that I was awake, August quickly rushed over and put a saddle underneath me so I could sit up.

"Aw...geeze...it's the love language all over again." Caleb said, watching August and I stare at each other.

"Shut up." Boone said, elbowing Caleb in the ribs but looking at me while rolling his eyes.

As my eyes focused on the scene in front of me, I looked back at my friends. I was flooded with relief. I had never felt so overjoyed. My family (or what was left of my family) was alive!

"I... I can't believe we all made it. The three of us!" I said with a shaky smile. Like it had been years since I had seen them.

Boone and Caleb looked at each other and then back at me, and grinned. We all started to laugh, and Boone stood and leaned down to give me a hug. "Your Pa was right. The

Lord works in mysterious ways. That's for sure!" he said as he gripped my shoulders with a gentle squeeze.

It was at that moment that I remembered what happened two days before. My relief and joy instantly turned sour, and I felt my stomach lurch and dread wash over me.

I immediately tried to stand up, trembling as I struggled to get to my feet. "We have to go… NOW… we have to go…… RIGHT NOW!" I stammered.

The Major spoke up. "Boy, sit back down and get some rest. Everything can wait until tomorrow."

'NO!' I snapped, catching everyone off guard. I slowly got up with the help of the saddle and fell on one knee. I forced myself back upright.

I frantically looked at both brothers. Caleb and Boone stared at me, confusion etched across their faces. "You don't understand! There is something over that knoll behind us that I escaped from! It's a chasm, I mean, the devils well or something like that! There are creatures, monsters, or something that lives in there! RIGHT UP THERE!"

Panicked, I looked at the Major and August, and then back to Boone and Caleb. Everyone stood still, staring silently at me. Moss stood up slowly and laid down his knife, cocking his head to peer at me, too. I felt the terror rising in my throat as I pointed frantically at the hillside in the distance.

"You don't understand! There is something over there behind us that I escaped from! It's a… cave… or… pit…. monsters… *creatures* live in there! They tied me to a post at the bottom and…" my words trailed off as I saw the expressions on their faces.

Caleb stood up and glanced down at Boone, then at August. August was staring at me intently with a slight frown on her forehead.

"Son... it will be alright," the Major said softly, gently placing his hand on my shoulder. "There isn't anything out there that none of us can't handle."

I brushed his hand aside. "You don't understand! None of you understand! We must leave NOW!" I shouted, trying again to stand on two feet.

"Reece!" Boone said, standing up beside Caleb. "Are you ok? Did you get hit on your skull or something? You had a large knot on the back of your head. That could possibly explain the dream...whatever you thought you saw."

I stopped. *He could be right. Maybe I did imagine all of this?* I shook my head.

"But what could have caused all these cuts and claw marks all over me?" I asked, looking at them. I lifted my shirt, flashing the bandages covering my stomach and back. August blushed, and looked away.

"Why, I noticed a bunch of briar patches on this mountain yesterday while I was getting some water. Bet you fell into one and knocked your head right out," answered the Major, slowly nodding his head. Boone and Caleb also nodded in agreement. August looked up and held my gaze for a few seconds, then looked down again and turned away.

I slowly sat back down. Maybe they were right. Maybe I imagined the whole thing.

The Major and August shuffled away, talking quietly to one another away from the campfire. Boone and Caleb sat back down a few feet away from me, and they too began to whisper to each other in hushed voices. Moss, who had finished cutting up the carrots and was boiling water over the fire, slowly walked toward me.

August walked back towards me, smiling a reassuring smile. She gestured towards Moss. "He helped me clean and dress your wounds."

"What's his name?" I whispered softly.

"Don't yet know. He doesn't answer any of our questions. Father and I think he's mute."

Not taking his eyes off me, Moss reached into his pocket and kneeled down right in front of me. He opened his hand to reveal my small pocket knife, which he placed in my right hand. I met his gaze and muttered, "Thanks." Moss simply gave me a small smile and stood, walking back towards to campfire. I looked down at the knife in my hand, and gripped it tightly in my fist.

What HAD happened to me?

ఴ

After supper, we sat around the small fire. The Major had fallen sound asleep with his back up against an old pine tree. Moss stared into the fire, not saying a word.

As August worked at scraping out one of the cooking pans a few feet away, I turned towards Boone and Caleb. "I killed Captain Patton's nephew."

Boone looked at me and replied, 'We know. Caleb found the Bowie knife sticking out of his chest."

"I…I didn't mean to. I thought both of you were…" My voice trailed off. "He attacked me right before the battle was over."

Both Boone and Caleb said nothing. August stopped cleaning and looked over at the three of us. Still holding the pan, she walked back over to the fire and said rather nonchalantly, "Well, er, sorry, but I couldn't help overhear. Father says it don't mean much if you're killing someone that's trying to kill you. The Bible says an 'eye for an eye.'"

I looked up at her. "No offense, but that don't really help me much," I replied, with more sarcasm than I intended. "What's the worst thing you ever did?"

She stopped and put down the pan. For a long moment, she stared at the fire and then sat down. She looked up and our eyes locked onto one another. No one spoke and it seemed as if the stars overhead were even enveloped more by the surrounding darkness.

Far off in the distance a lone wolf howled.

"One year ago, back in Shiloh, my company, the 101st of Second Corp, was being decimated. We were in full retreat. Running for our lives. You Rebs would wait and target only the officers wounding them in the legs so they couldn't run. When our men tried to rescue them, they too were picked off...one by one. Some were able to get to the wounded. Some weren't."

She then turned her head and like lightning bolts, her eyes bored into Boone and Caleb.

"What was left of our outfit jumped a small stone wall, with the gray coats right on our heels. Our flag barrier, I don't really remember his name, dropped the flag and you Rebs picked it up. Having lost many friends that morning... I couldn't stomach that. So, I jumped back over the wall and knocked an old Colonel off his horse. I then shot the Reb who stole our flag, jumped on to the Colonel's horse, cleared the wall and high-tailed it outta there with the stolen horse. In fact, it's the same horse I'm riding to this day."

She looked down at the pan she was scraping and poured some water on it from her canteen.

Boone looked over to me and mouthed, "What the…?"

I looked over at Caleb and his eyes were as big as saucers.

I returned my gaze to August, who looked at me and winked. Her green eyes danced mischievously in the campfire's glow.

"At least I got our flag back."

My God, I thought. *Who is this girl?*

I was starting to fall for her.

CHAPTER 31

The Onslaught

Around midnight, a stiff wind moved in from the north and it started to snow lightly. The Major and August brought out some extra blankets. I was feeling stronger, having rested and been fed, and I inched closer towards the fire to warm my face.

It was only a few hours later that I heard the first scream.

My eyes jerked open. A few seconds passed, and I heard a second and third scream. I sat up and looked around wildly. Boone, Caleb, and August began to stand, and I heard Caleb mutter, "What the hell…?"

Like lightning, Moss jumped instantly to his feet – much faster than any of us. He frantically scanned the fire's perimeter, a look of sheer terror flashing in his eyes. The snow began to fall in heavy tuffs blurring our vision and coating the ground.

"Father?" yelled August, loud and with an edge of panic in her voice. "*Father?!*" We looked at each other for a moment, and I could see the fear beginning to fill her eyes.

"Major? MAJOR!" I yelled out.

161

No response.

I hurried over to where the rifles were and grabbed the first one. Boone followed, and I quickly tossed him a rifle. He in turn tossed it to Caleb, who was on his heels. I handed Boone his rifle and kept the third for myself. August kept yelling for her father.

I looked over at the fire and saw Moss pull a small knife from his pocket, turning around with his back to the flame. Trying to see what was out there…beyond the light.

Boone, Caleb, and I checked that all three rifles were loaded. We turned and hurried back towards the fire. August raced over to where her supplies were and took out a large revolver. She quickly hurried back to us.

I looked over to where the horses were and caught sight of a mound of horse flesh and guts lying in piled puddles of blood.

My God, I thought. We didn't even hear the slaughter. The blood bath couldn't have been any quicker.

"Reece…what's out there? What have you seen?" August whispered, sidling up to me.

As I turned to answer her, I saw a shadow move from the darkness into the perimeter of the light. For the second time… it was revealing itself to me.

And it had the Major.

August's gaze followed mine. "Father… why you scared the ever-living daylight out of… me," she trailed off. She, like the rest of us, realized that something was not right.

The Major…he did not look…normal. He was still holding his book, and his face was frozen in a look of utter bewilderment. Blood was seeping out of his ears and eyes.

Behind him, sheltering in the pitch-black darkness was…
it. The thing that had chased me up the well and had nearly
caught me.

It would not reveal itself fully. A lopsided smile of jagged
teeth and a large bulbous head with red eyes was all that
I could see clearly. Its body, legs, and arms were cased in
shadows and appeared long, powerful, and leathery. One long
arm (or tentacle?) wrapped itself around the Major's waist,
with another holding up the Major's head. Its wings were
vibrating excitedly, like a bee at a flower.

It let out a low, soft hiss. It looked around from one
person to another. The Major still appeared to be alive.
I saw his eyes open and close as he slipped in and out of
consciousness.

After several tense seconds, it turned its gaze towards me
and stared at me for what seemed like a full minute. Nobody
moved. I don't think anyone remembered to even breathe.

It tilted its head at an angle, as if this…*thing*… had
a question to ask, and then quickly backed away into the
blackness from whence it came – carrying the Major with it.

"FATHER!" screamed August. She turned, looked at me
wildly, and then spun around to follow.

The three of us were right behind her.

"Watch for its tracks in the snow!" I yelled back at Boone
and Caleb as I raced after August. But as soon as the words
left my lips, I bumped into her. She had stopped dead in her
tracks.

She did not know where to go – the darkness was all-
consuming.

In a whisper, I hissed, "August, we need some light. Can't see a damn thing in this darkness and it won't be light for a couple more hours."

As if he read my mind, Moss immediately appeared holding two torchlights from the fire we left behind.

"Hurry!" August whispered desperately, grabbing a light. We shined the light down at the snow, and could now see the tracks.

It was headed back to the Devil's Well.

"Let's split up! Follow the tracks on all sides. It's headed that way…" I yelled, trailing off as I shined my torchlight ahead. "What the…?" The prints in the snow had disappeared.

It isn't snowing hard enough for them to be covered already, I thought.

Everyone stopped. August, Boone and Caleb scanned down and around to see if there were any more tracks, but none were found.

"Reece…what are we missing?" August asked, looking all around her.

I stood there, thinking. *It's not ahead of us, and it's certainly not behind us or we would have seen the back tracks…it couldn't be below us…*

"THE TREES. LOOK UP IN THE TREES!" I screamed.

We looked up, and there it was. I could see the silhouette of the Major's body, entangled in its grasp, dangling from high up in a pine tree. It hissed, and immediately jumped over to the top of another tree, dragging his limp body out of our light.

"I have a shot! I have shot," Caleb yelled, and immediately fired.

He missed.

The creature took another flying leap onto another tree. We ran after the beast as it glided from treetop to treetop. It was fast and we lost sight of it a couple of times, but the rustling of leaves and panicked scattering of birds helped us stay in close pursuit.

The sun began to slowly come up, and with dawn approaching, we could finally begin to make out the outline of the creature. The snow fell even harder, our chase up the mountain slowing.

My every muscle ached. I wanted to give up, turn around, run far from this place with my friends and forget this ever happened. But when I glanced over at August, I could see the panic and pain, tears staining her face as she screamed for her father.

I knew what was coming. By the grace of God, I had escaped. We had to try – for her.

"Reece!" Boone yelled, "Caleb and I will run ahead and try to stop him from going over the mountain! Flush him out our way!" With that, he and Caleb were gone. Blanketed by the heavy snowfall, they disappeared in the woods ahead. They were gone before I could even respond.

After a few minutes, August and Moss reached the top of the mountain with me right behind. They reached Boone and Caleb, who were staring straight ahead in shock and horror, frozen to the spot. There, standing on the precipice of the hole, stood the demon. As it turned toward us, it was now visible in its full glory.

Its smile never wavered; its eyes unblinking as it raised to its fullest stature. It brought to mind a praying mantis, long, lengthy legs with a body resembling a thin, emaciated man. The creature stood as tall as three or four men, and its Cheshire-smile revealed rows of sharp, jagged teeth. Before anyone could react, it turned quickly and jumped down into the cavity below. Horrified, Boone and Caleb raced forward, reaching the rim of the hole first. In unison, they spun around to face us, bewildered.

All thought it was gone.

They both started walking back towards the three of us, when suddenly the creature rose back up from the chasm with wings vibrating rapidly in the air, the Major held tightly in its mouth. Like a spider with prey in its web, it reached forward and grabbed both Boone and Caleb by their waists. And as if displaying trophies, it slowly lifted them up off the ground.

Boone didn't move. I didn't know if he passed out or … worse. Caleb desperately tried to stab the beast with his knife.

"SHOOT IT! KILL IT!' he yelled, panicked eyes pleading down at me.

I raised my rifle and fired.

The shot stuck the thing square in its forehead.

It wasn't fazed one bit. The bullet left a gaping hole between its eyes, and I watched in horror as black ooze dribbled out of the wound.

Then – unbelievably – the wound *immediately sealed itself back up.*

August fired her revolver right into its chest, over and over until the chamber emptied. Nothing. It didn't even flinch.

"Fire! We need the fire from the torches!" I screamed.

Moss shakily handed me one of the torches, and we exchanged a quick look. We then charged straight at the creature.

I saw it peer into the pit, and flick its eyes back at me. I looked at Caleb as he thrashed and screamed, and I will never forget his pleading eyes, begging for me to save him. Blood dribbled out of his mouth.

Never changing its expression, the creature looked at me in the eyes, turned, and jumped back down.

And it was gone.

CHAPTER 32
The Chase

The three of us stopped dead in our tracks. For several seconds, we stood rooted to the spot in stunned silence. August moved first, running to the rim of the hole with Moss and I on her heels. There was nothing to see but the empty void.

Absolute darkness.

I knew exactly where the stairs were, and for the second time and without another word, began the climb down into the grotto. August followed, holding the lighted torch.

For a moment, I didn't see Moss, but after several minutes, a glowing light from above indicated that he, too, was following. The three of us descended downward into the Devil's Well...to Nod.

We paused every so often and listened (hoping) for a voice, a noise, *anything*. But it was eerily quiet. We heard no sound, felt no breeze, and saw no light – aside from our own.

August eventually took the lead, with me following her and Moss bringing up the rear. She kept a relentless pace.

Every so often, one of us would trip or slip on the wet stairs, with the others reaching out to grab a jacket or collar and yank that person back onto the narrow path.

After what felt like hours into our descent, we came upon a small ledge. It was wide enough for all three of us to rest for a moment. August stopped here and muttered that we needed to take a quick break. We were breathing hard. I noticed that there was water running down the cavern walls, and with cupped hands Moss, collected enough water for each of us to take a drink.

August spoke for the first time, sitting down and rubbing her legs.

"Reece…what the HELL are we dealing with? What is that…*thing*?"

Despite everything going on at that moment, despite the terror and exhaustion and grief I was feeling, I couldn't help but think how absolutely beautiful she was as I looked into her eyes.

I tried to remain calm "I think it's some type of demon. I don't know much more than that." I didn't want to tell her the full story of what we were facing. Not yet.

I slid past, motioning for her and Moss to follow. We continued our pursuit.

Soon I caught sight of the all-too familiar glow from what I knew would be the small fire set in the middle of the cavern floor.

I couldn't put it off any longer. We stopped long enough for me to tell them both what happened to me in the days before. They looked at me incredulously, and I watched

August's eyes widen in shock and disbelief. She bit her lip, her mouth setting into a firm line of determination, as she stood up and pushed forward. "I'm gonna kill it," she said with a fierceness I had never heard before. "I'm gonna kill it and then I'm gonna burn it."

I don't need to worry about her, I realized. I was blown away by her grit, her bravery. I turned and followed her, continuing my steps downward.

We had finally arrived at the bottom. Sure enough, the small fire and wooden post were exactly as they were before. It was the same small room. August drew her pistol and Moss gripped his knife as I carefully stepped down on to the sandy floor.

Nothing. Nothing happened. *Not one damn thing.* There were no red eyes, no blow upon my head.

"What the....?" I whispered.

Looking for footprints, I lowered the torch and slowly walked around the room. There were none.

I looked over at August and she too had stepped on the cavern floor. We looked at each other with bewilderment.

Moss stood on the last step, scanning the area. He looked at me and then at August and, nodding his head, he too took the last step onto the floor.

Again… nothing happened.

Frantically, the three of us looked around and back at one another. The doorway! I quickly shined my light on to the walls of the room. They were course and rough. I noticed large scratch marks along the doorway as I scanned my light around until suddenly – the entranceway!

It was wide open.

"Here! They went through here!" I hissed in a hushed voice. I started towards the portal when I felt August put her hand on my shoulder. I turned to face her, her nose inches from mine.

She paused. "Sorry, my… er…. torch went out."

I swallowed, my mouth suddenly feeling dry. "That's… that's okay. Keep close," I whispered, hoping that she couldn't see my burning cheeks.

I turned back to face Moss, but he motioned for me to stop. He raised his knife and turned to face the cavern wall. With his knife, he carved an "X" on the stone blackened wall marking our path forward and for our return. I noticed that his torchlight was fading.

It was at that moment that it struck me that we might not return.

❧

The entryway appeared to be a long hallway of sorts. Our meager lights were not strong enough to reveal the ceiling height, but it appeared high enough for the beast. We walked a short distance before we came upon a large crack in the ground, a stone bridge crossing the gap. It started on our side and stretched across a blackened void, nearly 30 feet in length, leading to other side.

And there was a putrid, boiling stench emanating from the darkness below.

The passage led to a similar entryway across the bridge. I spotted a small ledge branching off the passage, running along the opposite wall which led to several large cave- like openings.

Stopping, I turned around. "It went through the main passageway for sure."

"How can you tell?" whispered August. I quickly walked over the bridge to the main entrance and, shining the light down, picked up the Major's glasses. I handed them to August, who was on my heels, and she placed them in her pocket with shaking hands. She wiped her eyes with the back of her glove and took a deep breath.

"Let's go,"

We crossed in single file. As I was first and had the brightest torch, I made it to the other side before the others.

It was then that I heard the voice.

"YOU'VE BROUGHT COMPANIONS. VERY GOOD."

Instantly, I froze.

I glanced back and it seemed like the others did not hear.

"WHY DON'T YOU TELL THE SOW THAT YOU WANT HER. YOU KNOW SHE WANTS YOU, TOO."

Embarrassed for both of us, I turned and yelled into the darkness.

"Shut up!"

August reached the end of the bridge, taking my hand as she stepped off and giving me a curious look. We just stared at each other for a moment before I looked away in shame.

"Come on…we gotta pick up the pace," I muttered as Moss joined us on the other side.

We walked in silence for a few minutes before it spoke again.

"GREECY REECEY. GUESS I WILL HAVE TO DANCE WITH SEVERAL OF THE OTHER BOYS TONIGHT!"

I staggered, nearly losing my footing and falling down. I stopped and shook my head to get him out. I took a deep breath as I stumbled forward, trying to keep moving, trying not to let it get to me.

"PA... PA... OH MY GOD, PA,"

"THERE....IS....NO....GOD....HERE....**BOY**!"

I said nothing and with determination kept walking.

An even-larger cavern loomed ahead, the stone path winding around one side and continuing onward. The trail seemed to be well-worn… with small fires burning on the ground every ten feet.

August and I exchanged glances as we tentatively began to walk the path. No one said a word, afraid to break the silence or else the terror might creep in and consume us.

And now there was a light emanating from above. It was not a blinding light but rather provided a soft moon-like glow. The path veered along the right side of the cavern, and about 10 to 15 feet to the left of the path it looked as if there was another hole. That area was pitch black.

"Reece… Reece... look up," I heard August whisper from behind me.

I turned around to look at both her and Moss. They both stared straight up, horrified expressions on their faces.

I followed their gaze and there, suspended in midair and slowly spinning around, were hundreds and hundreds of people. Dead. The bodies hung limp in midair, heads tilted obscenely backwards as if in prayer.

Praying or pleading for forgiveness.

August stood frozen in place; her eyes locked on the bodies above. "Sweet Jesus," she mouthed silently.

I swallowed hard, trying to steady my breathing. "Look for your father. We'll look for Boone and Caleb."

These poor souls. All the faces stretched upwards, as if pleading to God for redemption. They reminded me of Christ's crucifixion, arms outstretched.

Suddenly I heard August yell out. "Father!! Father!! Major Morgan! *DAD!*"

At that moment, all the faces of the people above in unison looked down at us.

I wanted to scream when I saw their eyes. Empty. Their faces showed no emotion, no recognition of any kind. It was as if their souls had been purged from their bodies, sheered away like excess wool from a sheep. If they could see us, they made no sound.

They were simply hollow shells.

"August, be quiet!" I hissed.

August gasped, covered her mouth, and frowned. "Okay, sorry… but we have to find them soon! Before it's too late!" she whispered back, pointing at the bodies above us.

Moss spotted them first. They, too, were floating above the ground. The three were displayed the same as the rest, heads tilted backwards and arms outstretched. The Major actually seemed to be at great peace, resting with eyes shut, still clutching his manuscript. A small amount of crusted blood was visible around his eyes and mouth. Caleb and Boone, however, seemed to be struggling to breathe. Like fish out of water, their chests heaved up and down as they gasped for air.

The process for them had not yet begun.

Moss ran over and motioned for me to climb on his shoulders. August helped boost me up, both of us moving as quickly as we could. I grabbed at Caleb, who was the lowest and most accessible.

His head immediately snapped forward as I grabbed his hand.

"Caleb... Caleb... it's me, Reece!" I whispered, shaking his arm. His lips parted, a small moan emanating from his mouth. His eyes focused as his head cleared.

"Reece... Reece?" he murmured, blood beginning to trickle out of his mouth. He gasped for air. "My ribs... they hurt... it hurts real bad," he groaned, still in midair.

"Caleb, I need for you to grab onto the Major's hand. Shake him awake like I did to you." I whispered, squeezing Caleb's hand.

Caleb weakly turned his head toward the Major and reached out and grasped his hand. The Major's head instantly jerked forward. He then turned towards Caleb.

"Major... Major... snap out of it! You have to wake up now!" I hissed, panic starting to creep into my voice.

His eyes became more focused, and as he looked down, his eyes locked with August's. He instantly recognized his daughter.

"Major, I need for you to reach out with your right hand and grab Boone... hurry!"

He turned and with his right hand reached up and took hold of Boone's left hand. Boone reacted much the same way as the other two. I slowly pulled Caleb, who in turn pulled the Major, who lastly pulled Boone down and toward the ground.

Holding Caleb tightly, I slowly lowered him to the ground. I had to pry his right hand from the Major's as he slipped in and out of consciousness. Bright red blood began once again to dribble out of his mouth.

I was kneeling beside Caleb when Boone touched the ground. He knelt for only a moment before standing shakily and then moved toward his brother. He knelt down and cradled Caleb's head. "Caleb… Caleb… it's me, Booney. I'm here, little brother!" he said between sobs.

Caleb did not respond, his breathing coming in short, ragged wheezes.

"Oh Caleb!" Boone cried out, weeping as he ran his fingers across Caleb's cheek. He laid his head onto his brother's chest. August knelt on the other side and stroked Caleb's hair, tears running down her cheeks. Caleb coughed, and opened his eyes slowly. He wiped his mouth with his sleeve and gave a small, pained smile.

"He's okay. He's okay!" I said, standing up quickly. I felt momentary relief flood my body, but then Moss tapped me on the shoulder and motioned that we needed to go.

As I helped Caleb stand, I looked over at the Major, who was staring upwards toward the people and the bright light emanating above them. "Come on, Father, we have to go," August pleaded, but it was as if he didn't hear her. He was lost in his own thoughts, mesmerized.

"Don't you see?" he mumbled. "It's…it's… the Dark… Expanse."

I lowered my voice and looked him in the eyes. "Major, we need to leave – now. There are things here that you haven't seen yet. Things that – if they catch you – will tear into your flesh and feed upon your bones! That Thing is out there – the shadow creature – whatever it is. The one that took you all down here. It will be back knowing that you have escaped. It will search for us with a vengeance. We need to go…NOW!"

Moss led the way. Boone held onto Caleb's side, supporting him as we began to hike back the way we came, guided by the one remaining, dim torchlight, the tinder having been singed off all the others. I followed behind them, helping Boone as needed, with August and the Major bringing up the rear. August gently led her father away from the light above and darkness below, and when I glanced back at them, I noticed the Major muttering to himself, over and over again. I could barely make out the words he babbled softly.

"It's the end… it's the end… it's the end… of days."

CHAPTER 33

The Escape

As we made our way out of the large cavern and down the small rock path, I heard the voice once again, growing louder in my mind with each chant. I looked at everyone else – no one seemed to hear the voice but me.

"You will never leave this place."

"YOU WILL NEVER LEAVE THIS PLACE."

"YOU WILL NEVER LEAVE THIS PLACE!"

We continued to stumble forward, making our way as quickly as we could across the darkened path. I looked back to see August clutching her father. Her gaze locked with mine for a moment, those iridescent eyes still managing to shine even amidst the horror happening around us. I squeezed Caleb against my side ever-so tighter, afraid to lose him again. He was now wheezing with every breath, and blood once again had started dribbling out of his mouth. He looked up at me.

"Leave me! You b...both need to leave me!" Caleb stuttered softly.

"Shut up Caleb!" snapped Boone, frowning and putting his finger to his lips.

Caleb smiled weakly, then winced in pain. "No, YOU shut up, Boone!"

We kept moving, struggling but staying on course, one step at a time. Eventually, we reached the stone bridge. I bumped into Moss, who had stopped directly in front of the bridge.

"Why have we stopped? WHY have we stopped? We have to KEEP going!" August yelled from behind me, panic in her voice.

I motioned to Boone, who took hold of Caleb as I gently let go, making sure he was not going to fall. I turned around and stepped forward, craning to look around Moss.

The shadow creature. This demon from hell stood on the other side of the stone bridge. It was squatting, waiting – and staring right at us. Its gaze bore right through me, and I felt it down to my bones. A chill ran through my body as my heart began to beat furiously against my chest.

"Shit!" I said softly to no one. I swallowed, and took a step forward. Moss put his hand on my shoulder and motioned that he would go alone to face this creature.

As he proceeded to draw out his knife, the creature reared up and shook its misshapen head from side to side. Then it lifted a hand and pointed directly at me.

Me. It wanted *me*.

I looked over at Moss and then back at Caleb, Boone, and August. The Major appeared to be in shock and showed no emotion.

"It wants me," I said evenly. "I guess I knew that, for some unknown reason, it only wanted me."

I looked again at August, who had tears streaming down her face. "No!" she screamed. "I'll do it!" She started towards me, but Boone put his arm up and stopped her.

"I'm bigger than both of you, so I'll go!" shouted Boone, glancing at August then turning to face me.

But before he could do anything, I grabbed the knife from Moss's hand and stepped on to the stone bridge. It was slippery from the moisture in the air. The creature started pacing from side to side, its gaze never wavering. We stared at one another for a few moments.

I took a deep breath and sprinted as fast as I could towards him, full speed. The creature made a loud screech, and did the same from the other side.

At that moment, I thought of my father. The one who raised me despite his shattered dreams. I thought about how his life had been cruelly taken from him. I thought of Captain Patton, and Black Damp McCabe, and all of the brutality inflicted by him.

I felt the anger I'd been holding back scream through my body, a rage like I'd never known before. For the second time, I didn't care if I lived or died. The fire in my belly burned too hot.

As we neared one another, we both started slipping and sliding on the moist bridge. The creature struggled to stay upright as he barreled towards me.

In an instant, I realized that this was my opportunity.

The distance between the two of us quickly narrowed until suddenly, I was upon it. As it reached for me, I slid down and across the stone of the bridge between its legs. I stabbed wildly above me as I slid, slicing off a portion of the creature's right leg. The beast let out a piercing scream and tried to turn around, but the bridge was too small and the stones too wet. Now behind it, I was able to grab onto its right wing and pull myself up to stand. Both wings began to flutter as the creature tried to fly.

But I held on.

I took the knife and with a wild frenzy carved large slits into both of the wings. It frantically struggled in my grasp. As the creature tried to turn towards me, I stood firm and pushed it over the side of the bridge with all the force I had left.

Its left limb grabbed ahold of the side of the bridge. I gazed over the side into the darkness and saw it hanging, struggling to hold on. I knelt down, never taking my eyes off of it. Its eyes locked with mine as it twisted frantically around, but it never pleaded, never wavered, and never showed any signs of emotion.

I took the knife and began to cut through the only limb holding the creature on the bridge.

Matching its stare, I hissed, "You can go to Hell. Oh, that's right...you're already there."

And with that the creature, the beast from this pit of darkness and horror, fell into the blackness below.

CHAPTER 34

Upward

As I stood up, I felt August's hand on my shoulder. I turned and faced her, those eyes of hers shining as she looked into mine. I brushed a bit of her hair from her face, and she took my hand in hers and pressed it against her cheek. We both stood still for a moment, staring sheepishly at each other. Boone marched up with Caleb under his arm. He grinned and winked at me before leaning in and saying, "Break it up, Romeo – we're not out of the woods yet."

"Yea, Romeo, not out of the woods yet," echoed Caleb with a ragged breath.

A blush crept up August's face as she smiled, turning to retrieve her father who was still standing by Moss. She gently led him across the bridge. I waited until they walked by, Moss following behind them. I gave him a wry smile before handing him back his knife.

For a moment, he just stared at me before pulling me gently to his shoulder in a hug. We stood there for only a moment when he let me go, and then looked down at where the creature's arm was still dangling from the side of the bridge. We looked at one another and he kicked it with his foot.

The severed arm fell down into the blackness below.

ᐈ

Moss took the lead and I brought up the rear as we followed the marked trail, snaking back the way we came. By the light of our small torch, we managed to find our way back to the entry cavern.

We rested only for a moment for Caleb. Boone took off his over shirt and tore off both sleeves, wrapping up Caleb's ribs. He was able to stand more easily and even place some weight on that side of his body.

The Major seemed to be in somewhat of a trance. He looked at me and suddenly spoke. "Abandoned all hope, you who enter here. Where the souls who in life could not commit to either good or evil now must run in a futile chase after a blank banner, day after day, while hornets bite them and worms lap their blood."

He stopped and turned to August, a tear running down his cheek. He wiped it away with the back of his hand. "I am so very sorry for bringing you along in this cursed venture. What was I ever thinking?"

"Father, we'll get out of this yet," she replied, taking him by the hand. She glanced over to me.

We hadn't rested for more than five minutes before I saw a pair of those cursed red eyes. I swallowed hard, peering ahead.

"Reece…Reece…what is it?" August asked in a whisper, her eyes wide as she looked at me.

I stared into the blackness. Maybe my eyes were playing tricks on me. I was so tired.

It was then that I saw not two red eyes glaring at us, but now four.

"We have to move! NOW! The things with red eyes are here!" I shouted. "Go…GO! Everyone head for the stairs and climb! August, get your father up the stairs NOW!"

I grabbed Caleb and with Boone's help rushed him to the granite stairs while August helped the Major. As they started to scramble up the stairs, I turned around and saw hundreds of red eyes rushing into the room from the opened passageway beyond.

Moss stood by the fire with the only torch we had remaining, fumbling as he tried to relight the end. I ran over to him and pulled him away just as his torch lit, and both of us followed Boone and Caleb up the stone steps.

"Don't stop! Don't anybody stop! We will hold them back as best as we can!" I screamed.

Moss handed me the torch and drew out his knife. We hurried backwards up the stairs – I with the torch, swinging it from side to side, and Moss slashing at anything that got close.

The room now was quickly filling up. The red-eyed creatures were always careful to stay out of the light, but they were agile enough to run up the side of the cavern walls. Every time Moss would slash at the ones above, several would stab and claw at his legs. No sooner would I lower the torch to draw them off when one or two would pounce on my back or throw themselves at my chest or face.

After some time, I noticed two things. First, the firelight below was becoming smaller. It was either fading away as we were getting further away or it was going out. Second, Caleb was wheezing and coughing up more blood the further we climbed. I didn't know how much farther he could go.

Our torchlight, too, was beginning to fade. I looked up and saw a small ledge where we could rest for a moment, just a moment to catch our breath. Moss and I would try to hold these things at bay the best we could.

I yelled, "August, hold up on that ledge before you!"

She did as I instructed, and with Boone's help, they dragged Caleb onto the ledge and propped his back against the cavern wall. Both Moss and I stopped at the stairs below and fended off any of the red eyes that got to close.

We did not rest very long. The creatures kept multiplying, and I could see them scaling the opposite side of the cavern in an attempt to head us off from above.

"Would you look at that?" yelled the Major, pointing. "They move in unison, as if a collection of one thought, or one mind!"

Boone reacted first. "Caleb can't take much more! Reece – lift him up and put him on my back! I will carry him the rest of the way!" he yelled, snapping me out of the fog I was in, watching those things crawl and slither up the walls. I handed Moss the torch and lifted Caleb onto Boone's back. He was very pale and limp. Blood soaked the side of his mouth and collar. August steadied Boone and turned to her father, leading him forward and up, resuming the climb.

My arms were now starting to ache. Moss – unbelievably – showed no signs of fatigue.

I noticed a small light illuminating from above. It was the entrance! *Thank God*, I silently prayed.

I patted Moss's shoulder and he glanced up and saw the light. A wide grin spread across his face.

August yelled from ahead. "The light… the light… I see light!"

CHAPTER 35
My God... NO!

It was as if seeing that light above us renewed our strength. We were nearly there. God's light! We'd made it!

As we reached the opening of the hole, the glow became brighter, and the red eyes, the creatures from below, stopped their attacks. It also became much colder. I could see the sunbeams shining into the cavern, small flakes of falling snow starting to dance in the light.

Finally, after what seemed like an eternity, August and her father reached the top and disappeared. With none of the red-eyed things in pursuit, both Moss and I were able to help carry Caleb the rest of the way.

Boone was the next one out, and he collapsed on to the solid ground, which by this time was covered by about eight inches of freshly fallen snow. Moss and I, carrying Caleb carefully, exited together, nearly tripping over Boone, who was lying face up in the snow. The expression of joy on his face nearly made Moss and I laugh. It seemed to be late evening, as the sun was just beginning to creep behind the mountains running across the far horizon and the valley below.

We gently placed Caleb down for a quick rest – it was clear to all that he could go no further. After a moment, August yelled to us to make our way back to the camp we had made before this horror had started. She searched for dry kindling to start a fire, while the Major rested against a tree.

Gently lifting Caleb up again, we did as we were told. Within 15 minutes, Caleb was laying by a roaring fire and his pulse was steady. He appeared to be sleeping.

I sat there, watching Caleb rest in the fire's glow. *I did it. I destroyed the demon, we are all here together, and we are safe,* I thought to myself, finally feeling like I could take a deep breath. The first time I felt at peace in days.

Boone and I prepared a small shelter from the snow. We took a fairly large, low lying branch from a large pine tree nearby and bent it to the ground. There we hooked it around a much lower branch. We then were able to find large, broken-off branches on the ground underneath several other large trees (where the snow had not built up) and proceeded to lean these along the bent branch piling the snow on top of the broken branches. This made for a dry, but snow-covered roof.

As August cleared out the floor of the makeshift lean-to, her father carried over our snow-covered provisions that we had left the night before. Moss, meanwhile, constructed a tripod out of branches, boiled up water, and cut up some of our food to make stew.

All was quiet and all was calm.

As the night's darkness crept in, and before our meager supper for the night, I walked back up to where the entry of the hole was to track down several large rocks. I knew that if I put them in the fire, they would heat up nicely and I could put them into the lean to. They would keep us warm for the night. I took a large stick from nearby and a very torn shirt that I had in my satchel. I wrapped it around the stick and made a small torch, which I lit with the fire.

The snow had apparently stopped during our construction of the shelter, and as I approached the hole's entrance, I found our point of exit.

My mind started screaming. *DON'T go over to the ledge and look down!* For a moment, I resisted the urge, but I decided that my fear would not get the best of me. I slowly walked over to the side and stared down to the emptiness below.

Nothing.

I told myself that all would be well through the night. The creature was no more. We needed to rest and recover. Caleb couldn't trek through the snow at night in his condition, and every one of us was exhausted. So I swallowed down my fear, walking over to where I had seen several large rocks under an old tree and gathered them into my arms. I retraced my steps back to the campsite and placed the stones into the fire for heating.

We sat huddled around the fire, eating the stew and sipping heated snow water. All of us remained silent. Despite the exhaustion weighing on us all, I still felt that someone should keep watch. I finally broke the silence, explaining my concerns.

Boone chuckled. "I don't think that's necessary. While you were getting the rocks, I set up several spring snares around that side of the camp. Anything coming in from that side, the snare will snag them and make a snapping noise."

"Nonetheless, I would feel better if we take watches throughout the night," I replied, frowning. August and her father agreed, and Moss also nodded in agreement. I volunteered to keep the first watch and Boone (with some reluctance) agreed to take the second.

As everyone bedded down for the night, all remained unnervingly quiet. I had placed the rocks in the middle of the lean-to about an hour before, so it felt warm and comfortable. Everyone drifted off to sleep except the Major and I. He was leaning up against the back wall of the lean-to with eyes closed when he softly spoke.

"And when they shall have finished their testimony, the beast that ascendeth out of the bottomless pit shall make war against them, and shall overcome them, and kill them," he murmured, before opening his eyes and looking at me.

He then said nothing more as we both watched August's chest slowly rise and fall in slumber.

With a sigh, he said, "She's got an affection for you. She hasn't been around boys of your age much since the war started. Her mother died years ago and since then it's been just her and I."

"I, em…. I also…. I…" I fumbled to find words, but he interrupted me before I could finish. "No, don't say anything…just listen," he said, leaning forward to look at me closely.

"If something happens to me. If I was to be killed in battle, or taken prisoner, or die at the hand of that thing, please promise me you'll take good care of her. I would be very proud if it were you that she'd end up being with. You've got a certain…quality."

I looked down – I didn't know what to say.

Several more minutes passed before I broke the silence.

"Major, what did we stumble into?"

Eerie shadows danced across his face from the small camp-fire outside as he slowly answered.

"I…really don't know. It's all so…unbelievable. Your guess is as good as mine. Dante's Inferno, Hells Gate, The End of Eternity…take your pick. Any way you look at it we…are… lost," he said softly, looking down at his hands, which were shaking slightly. He blew on them to warm them up and then hid them behind his back.

And then the most unbelievable thing happened. The escape slave named Jupiter Moss… spoke.

"It be from the Enchiridion." With eyes glowing, he quietly continued. "It be the beast from the Bible."

I said nothing. *What was there to even say?* After that, both the Major and Moss fell quickly into an uneasy sleep.

✦

At around midnight, I peered out from our cozy shelter and saw that the snow had started to fall in large chunks again. The wind started blowing out of the northeast, creating an unnerving howl from the trees above. Not long after, I heard a snap from across the campfire, which had now emitted a soft glow, and then a loud screech.

Apparently, the screech wasn't loud enough to wake anyone else. I got up from where I sat and positioned myself near the entrance of our lean-to. We had made a small "door" out of sticks and brush, but I was able to peer outside with one eye.

I saw a large shadow pass by slowly, and it seemed as if something was sniffing the ground. When it reached the door, I remained frozen, my heart beating fast in my chest, imagining the worst. Whatever it was hesitated for only a moment. I caught a glimpse of its breath, highlighted by the campfire, as it rose up and disappeared into the cold air. I couldn't get a good look, but whatever it was remained in camp for only about a minute or two before meandering away.

It's probably a wolf, I thought to myself as my mind raced. *Probably just a wolf.* I stayed awake, rooted to the spot for the remainder of the night and did not wake Boone, who had his arm over Caleb in a dead slumber, a slight drool dribbling out of his mouth. As dawn broke over the eastern sky, I got up and exited our little shelter.

We're safe in the light, I said to myself as I stretched my legs and walked over to where the fire had been to clear off the snow. In doing so, I noticed tracks leading from where the hole was located, through our campsite, and leading off in the opposite direction. I felt a dread pulse through my body. Hearing a noise, I snapped my head around, my eyes darting back and forth, but it was just Moss exiting the lean-to. He stretched and nodded to me. He was followed by August, whose long black hair was slightly disheveled, cheeks pink in the cold air. She looked absolutely beautiful in the early morning sun.

I walked over to them both. "We had a visitor last night, but I couldn't tell what it was because it was too dark." I pointed to the tracks in the snow. We all looked down, no one saying a word.

August finally exhaled, and spoke softly. "The tracks appear to be too small for that…thing. Anyway, we saw you push him off the stone ledge. Nothing could have survived a fall like that." She tried to sound sure of herself, but I could hear the uncertainty in her voice. She looked away, gazing across the clearing and towards the woods.

Moss said nothing. I was getting ready to tell him I heard him talk but before I could speak, he turned to me and motioned for us to get small sticks and brush to make a fire with. August looked back at Moss, and then at me. She flashed up a gentle smile and I reached to brush my finger across her cheek. For a moment, I felt like I could take her into my arms and kiss her lips again, but I hesitated. She touched my finger at her cheek and turned to Moss. "Yes, let's get a fire on. We need to get the coffee going before anyone else wakes up."

Moss wandered off in the direction of the hole and both August and I slowly walked in the opposite direction. As we departed camp, we were finally alone for a moment. I took her hand in mine and we walked together, side by side. She looked at the ground as we walked, searching for dry twigs and brush, but I couldn't stop staring at her.

We both stopped walking altogether and turned to face one another. I couldn't wait another second. I reached down and with both hands, took her face in my palms and gently kissed her lips. My heart was pounding so intensely that I thought it would physically break through my chest. She returned my kiss, and when we broke apart, she smiled and ran her fingers through my hair. She pulled me close to her chest and we stood there, in each other's embrace, for what felt like a long time.

From that moment on, we never left each other's side.

As we broke our embrace, August stepped to her right, nearly stumbling over a very weathered, large grey rock. It was partially covered in moss with several large cracks running up the middle. I started to chuckle, however, I quickly stopped when I noticed August was not laughing at all.

"Reece, look here" she said, peering at the boulder. She knelt down to look closer. With both hands, she gently started peeling away the moss and soon we both recognized what appeared to be some type of chiseled-out lettering.

MALUM NO ES HIC

"What is this? How could this be here?" she replied, staring at the whittled letters. I bent down and gently ran my fingers across each letter, wondering what they meant.

"Wait! I know... I know!" she gasped, turning her head and looking at me. "It's Latin. But it's missing two letters. See? Here... and here," August pointed as she spoke. "You can barely see where these two letters were etched. Both the "n" here and the "t" have been so worn down, they're nearly unrecognizable."

"What's it mean?" I asked, wishing that I would have paid more attention to my father's English class.

August frowned for a moment. "It actually reads...

Malum non est hic

As the words left her lips, August bolted up, almost as if shot. "We need to get back to camp. NOW!"

As she started to run, I grabbed her and turned her around to face me.

"What does it mean?"

She looked into my eyes and replied:

"There is evil here."

We were about 50 feet from the camp when we heard the first scream.

The same scream I had heard the night before.

"Shit, shit, shit… no… NO!" I yelled, beginning to run. August was already a few steps ahead of me. As we burst into camp, all hell had broken loose!

The creature! The demon! It was standing in the middle of the camp, and it had the Major, Boone and Caleb in its grasp. It was shaking them violently from side to side!

And its leg. The leg that I had chopped off had fully grown back.

Moss had positioned himself in between it and the path to the cavern. He waved a fiery torch, trying to block its way back to the cavern and blackness below.

"Over here… OVER HERE!" I screamed at the beast, but it wouldn't take its eyes off of Moss. The creature, carrying the Major, Boone and Caleb limply in its clutches, moved towards Moss. As easily as swatting a fly, it batted him away. With a simple swipe, Moss was airborne, smashing into the trunk of a tree.

He crumpled, and didn't move.

As quick as lighting, the creature raced towards the cavern. August and I ran as fast as we could but its strides were much longer than ours and he was easily able to outdistance us.

We kept running, slipping in the snow, pushing tree limbs and brush out of our way as we moved through the woods. I could hear the creature screeching ahead of us, and my heart beat frantically as I used every ounce of strength left in my body to *just run.* Suddenly, we were there, bursting through the trees, finally reaching the cavern wall. There the creature stood, and once again, it turned to face us.

"NO!" I yelled, bending over with my hands on my knees as I sucked the cold air into lungs. I looked up, looking the creature in the eyes. "TAKE ME! TAKE ME! I'M THE ONE YOU WANT!"

The creature seemed to hesitate. I could hear August behind me crying. "Nooooo... FATHER!"

The creature paused for a moment longer before it broke my gaze. It then turned and, once again, leapt into the darkness below.

I screamed until my lungs felt raw. *Not again, my God, not again!*

August and I ran up the knoll. When we got to the top, to where the hole was, to where the steps led downward, we stopped. We were faced with nothing but a field of snow.

The hole was gone.

CHAPTER 36

Damaged

We sat in stunned silence, while thick snow fell around us like white dogwood petals. August's eyes looked up at me, pleading, begging me to find a way back into the cavern and save her father.

But there was nothing that I could do. In one fell swoop, I had lost all that remained of my family. Boone and Caleb… the two people who meant the most to me in this world… were gone. Just like that.

August began to sob uncontrollably, head in her hands. I stood up and walked over to where the stone steps would have led downward.

There was nothing to see but snow-covered grass.

All hope was lost.

YOU WILL NEVER LEAVE THIS PLACE!

I WILL FIND YOU!

YOU WILL NEVER LEAVE THIS PLACE!

For a moment, I just stood there, breathing in the cold air in a daze. I could not shake the voice out of my skull. I rose slowly, pounding my fists against my head.

Moss walked over and gently grabbed both my hands.

"Master Reece, we gots to go."

"Ahhhh, once again you can talk,' I snapped, angrily. "Don't call me master. I am a master of nothing!"

Moss said nothing. He turned and walked back to August, who had stopped crying and sat silently as if in shock. He gently stood her up, allowing her weight to lean against his sturdy frame.

Moss led August over to me and stood behind me, not knowing what to do next. I stood up, exhaling and unsteady on my feet for a moment. After I regained my composure, the three of us walked back down the knoll and through the forest, back to the makeshift camp we had constructed the night before.

Shattered.

"We need to get the hell off this godforsaken place NOW!" I snapped, picking up some of the supplies we had left the night before.

"If we are to make it down, we have to go now because it will be dark soon. Let's pack what we have and at least get down this mountain, away from this cursed place before nightfall. We can camp beside Sam Black Church then make our way west to my father's and my... er... I mean, my house – if it's still standing."

August turned her gaze to me, her eyes rimmed with tears and exhaustion. I gently took her hand and placed it in mine.

She nodded her head in agreement. We all stood, exiting the shelter and grabbing what we could find in the snow.

The descent was far easier than expected. The snowfall on top of the mountain was much deeper than what had fallen down below. However, it was bitter cold. The frosted air stung our cheeks as we made our way down the other side of the mountain, the opposite of the direction that we had climbed up, all separately before fate brought us together. This side of the mountain provided a more commanding view of the valley below and of the mountains beyond.

Every so often, either August or I would trip and slide, but we were always able to grab hold of a tree limb or something to stop our fall.

Moss, on the other hand, seemed at ease on the mountain, and not once did I see him slip or fall. Instinctively and without effort, he would weave or jump over a large boulder or fallen tree. He led the way, with August and I trailing behind. Every so often, I glanced back over my shoulder, scanning for anything following.

I saw and heard nothing.

Around nightfall, we arrived at the base of the mountain. We were spent. Our failed attempts at rescue in the days and nights before had taken their toll. We started toward the main road, leading to both Cucumber and beyond to Beckleyville, but we didn't get very far. We decided to stop under a large grove of pine trees, where the snowfall was light. Moss and I – once again – manufactured a rough lean-to out of a large fallen branch and covered it with smaller branches and pine needles.

We huddled in for the night.

We dared not make a fire.

ⷮ

It was around midnight. I couldn't sleep, so I was awake, staring out of our shelter into the darkness when I saw movement in our little area of the woods. Remaining very still and not wanting to wake the others, I watched as something wandered dangerously close.

I slowly reached over to where August slept and grabbed the pistol lying beside her, and I waited.

And waited.

This time I'll kill it and then make SURE it's dead, my mind raced.

As the it slowly approached, I quickly sprang up, screaming at the top of my lungs. Raising the gun up to fire, I received a full spray of the most suffocating, putrid stink I'd ever smelled.

The… creature voiced a loud hiss and quickly scampered away. It left me standing there, stinking to high heaven. Moss and August quickly jumped up by my side, but then as quickly, covered their faces and hustled out of the shelter.

"Lord be, what's that smell?" laughed Moss, looking me up and down.

I looked helplessly over at August, who had a hand up, holding her nose. Chuckling, she replied, "That, my good sir, was a skunk…and a mighty fat one at that."

I stepped outside, trying to wave the scent off of me. They both backed away, and August stifled a laugh as she pointed at the shelter. "Don't think you're sleeping in here tonight!"

Moss hid a smile. "Mister Reece, I'll get you a blanket and perhaps you could keep watch for the remainder of the night. Outside."

CHAPTER 37
The Trip Home

The sun almost seemed to rise earlier than usual, and brought with it a bright, sunny day with not a cloud in the sky. Hungry, tired, and cold, the three of us got moving as soon as we awoke, traveling in a southwest direction around noon.

Moss and August insisted that I travel downwind and keep my distance of about 20 feet.

We came upon the Beckleyville Road around lunchtime. The road seemed empty of recent travel, and where we came out of the woods, the surrounding grassland appeared barren and desolate. There was not as much snow here, so before moving on, we examined for any signs of fresh wagon tracks or footprints. Finding none, we proceeded onward to Sam Black Church.

No one spoke much. Every once in a while, I turned around to make sure that nothing followed. I stared back at the Five Finger Mountains, towering in the distance – it seemed to always appear blanketed in a halo of fog.

Lord, how I missed them. My heart ached for them. There were times during our trek home that I felt physically sick for them.

Nothing that happened made any sense. I tried to understand, to find something that could explain what just happened. I repeated the events over and over again in my mind while walking home.

I blamed myself for not understanding.

It was my selfish, vengeful pride that led them to a most certain and predictable death. There was a large part of me that died with them on top of that mountain.

I was also the cause of my father's death. We never would have gone to that dance if not for me. And for what? To satisfy a self-centered desire?

I should have been the one taken.

I should have been the one selected by that foul, abominable thing.

It should have been me.

Eventually, we came across that tired old pine tree where we had cut down Jed Anderson's body. I insisted that we stop and left the road to find his grave.

Finding the small mound covered with stones I knelt, and as the others stood by, said a small prayer.

As I stood up, August sidled up beside me and tenderly asked, "Who was he?"

"My friend," I replied softly. For several seconds, the three of us stared at the grave and then we turned, almost in unison, and continued our trek homeward.

❧

203

Several hours later, we finally reached the old stone church. Burnt down long ago (some say by a preacher who had gone mad) the stone remnants reminded me that it was only a week or so ago that we stopped here and made camp. It was here that we met Captain Patton.

I told Moss and August to go around back to find the small fire pit, hoping that there may be some kindling still available to burn. Together, they started a fire. Meanwhile I discovered a creek located about 100 yards along the back of the church. Taking my satchel in my hands, I wandered over to a small pool of water nestled in the creek bed. I stripped off the foul-smelling clothes and using a torn shirt dipped it into the cold creek water and quickly washed myself. The effect was immediate and stimulating. It seemed to snap me out of my sadness and sorrow. I used the mud in the water to scrub myself clean and rinsed off with the wetted rag. I left the stinking clothes by the creek and put on a dirty, but dry, shirt and pants.

I quickly ran back to the fire and grabbed my blanket. "Now that's much better," August said with a smile as she took my hand.

No one said anything for several minutes until Moss spoke, puncturing the silence. Looking deeply into the fire, he quietly said, "I be an escaped slave from Virginia."

"I pretty much gathered that," I said, looking at him. He was hunched over, and for the first time since we met, appeared small and unsure of himself. "You do not have anything to fear from us."

August looked at me and then at him. She smiled. "You're one of us now."

I smiled back at her, looking at her as I spoke to the both of them. "Moss, you stood with us when most men would have run away. It would be a privilege if you – both of you – would stay with me at my house… if it's still standing, that is."

Tearfully, August nodded, and then said softly, "Okay."

Moss said nothing for a long moment. He then looked at both of us and said, "You all… you need to know what I done. I killed a man."

He paused but then continued, softly and more to himself than us. "But he needed killen! Lord knows, he needed killen."

We said nothing. We didn't need to. He knew that we both understood.

He then stood up, looked at us straight on, and proudly introduced himself to us as Jupiter Moss.

For about two hours on that cold November night, he told us his story. He told us of the cruelness of humanity. The evilness that infected men. And at the end, he told us that he believed that what we went through, that what had happened nights and days before, well… was God's revelation.

CHAPTER 38

Home

The next morning, we woke up hungry and cold. The coffee and food ran out the night before. Cucumber was still three or four days ahead, so we gathered up our remaining supplies and continued our journey home.

It was approaching the middle of the day when we heard the first of several horses approaching. Not sure who they were, we hid behind a fallen tree about 30 feet from the road.

There we waited.

A few minutes later, three confederate riders galloped past, racing like bats out of hell. I looked over at August, who shrugged. After they rode by, we waited several minutes before proceeding on.

It was like that for next three days. Men, horses, and cannon, all in Confederate gray, were apparently in a fast retreat from the town of Lewisburg. We kept hidden whenever we heard them approach, making sure none could see us. We drank from nearby streams and ate raw crawdads fearing that a fire would draw in unwanted visitors. As we neared Cucumber, I began to recognize the all-too familiar landscape.

But it had changed.

We passed burnt-out homes and barns, some still smoldering, deep orange embers and charcoal-black smoke a stark contrast against the white snow. There were dead cows and sheep laying in fields, crows and buzzards feeding on their rotted carcasses. The smell of death stung my nose, making my stomach heave.

We finally, *finally* rounded the last curve in the road to where my house was. Using every last bit of the remaining energy I had, I took off at a dead run. I stared ahead as I ran, feeling my chest tighten as I said a prayer under my breath until suddenly, there it was. The house, the one on Little Dog Lane, where my father and I lived for so many years…. had survived.

I stood there for a moment, catching my breath and feeling the tears well up in my eyes. August and Moss walked up on either side of me, and August took my hand in hers and gave it a squeeze. I looked down at her, and for the first time in what felt like forever, felt, well, *safe*.

Together, the three of us walked home.

As we stepped onto the front porch, I noticed that several of the windows had been broken. As we moved into the foyer, I could tell immediately that the home had been ransacked. Furniture was missing or knocked over. The kitchen was a mess, most of the dishes missing or broken in shards on the ground. All of Pa's books were scattered across the floor, a sea of ripped paper and torn bindings. August stepped gingerly over the mess, not stepping on a single page. I watched as she leaned down and picked up Pa's Bible – many of the pages ripped out – and closed it carefully, placing it back on the shelf.

Watching her do this made something deep within my heart fall in love with her even more.

I walked upstairs to Pa's room. It appeared to be untouched, but it was obvious that someone had slept in the bed. My room upstairs also remained untouched – other than my overturned bed. The windows in both my room and my father's room remained intact.

As I stood there staring, I could see Moss out of my window, walking across the yard and into our small barn. He emerged a few moments later, carrying some dry wood to start a fire.

I walked back down the stairs and found August in the kitchen. Together, we both started to clean up the mess in front of us. August began to open up all the cupboards, and discovered that all the food had been removed.

Turning to face me, she said, "Reece, what are we going to do about food?"

"We need to look in the cellar. My father always covered the door with a small rug just in case of some type of emergency. Normally, the dining room table stood over top of the rug, but it's gone," I said, pointing to the rug in the dining area slightly off of the kitchen.

August and I took two of the corners and threw back the carpet, exposing the cellar door. It did not seem to have been opened. I inserted my fingers into two notches made along the side of the door and lifted.

It would not budge.

I cursed in frustration, but felt August's hand on my back. She knelt down beside me, sliding her fingers into one side while I took the other. Both of us lifted as hard as we could. Slowly, *slowly* the door began to open. I peered down into the cellar, my eyes adjusting to the darkness.

It was stocked full of food, clothing, and blankets.

All saved by my father.

I smiled to myself as August looked down into the cellar. She squealed with joy. As she climbed down to explore further, she looked back up to me, eyes shining with excitement and relief. "I really, really like your father."

As I helped her up from the cellar, we heard Moss call out. "Reece, you'll want to see this."

August and I stepped outside, following Moss into the yard. He led us to the large oak tree on the left side of the house by about 50 yards.

As I walked up to that tree, I saw where someone had buried my father.

I stood still, not even daring to breathe at first. I stared down. A small cross had been built out of old barn siding, and his name was carved deep into the wood. Later, I had the cross removed and replaced it with a stone headstone with his full name, date of birth, and death. Below the dates I also had engraved: *Have Faith and the Way Will Open.*

Later, I also constructed headstones for Boone, Caleb, and August's father. Having these imitation graves somehow comforted me.

As I stared down, August reached up with both hands and gently turned my head to hers and kissed me. "I understand," she said softly. As I looked at her, I saw the tears of her own grief beginning to slip down her cheek. I took her into my arms, resting my chin on the top of her head for a moment. I moved back, meeting her eyes with mine again. So much passed unsaid between us at that moment. We both now knew what tremendous loss does to a person, digging out a hole of grief, never to be fully closed…never to just *disappear* and leave behind nothing but a blanket of new-fallen snow.

Where do we go from here?

August touched my cheek. "Stay here. Moss and I will make supper. Come inside when you're ready."

With that, she and Moss walked back to the house. I slowly knelt down by the foot of Pa's grave and cried.

As I wept, I spoke to him. I told him everything that happened since his death. It poured out of me like water from a bucket. I told him about Black Damp, about Captain Patton, about August and her father. In doing so, I felt as if maybe Boone and Caleb were also with him, listening and laughing. How I shall miss both of them, the laughs, our friendship, even our little game of Mumblety-Peg. I stayed there until night began to fall and then rose, said my good-byes, and walked back to the house.

ᐧᐧ

We stayed at the house from that night forward, August, Moss, and myself. Imagine, a rebel, Yankee, and former slave all living under one roof. Working together. Until the war was over, we each assumed our roles, each playing a part in our little makeshift family that we created. After the war ended,

Moss became more visible in the community. Every Sunday he would make us put our finest clothes on and go to church. In this church, most of the parishioners were former slaves. There, we took in the sermon and watched as Moss sang loudly in the choir. Once church ended, we traveled back home and the three of us would prepare a dinner and then rest and reflect for the rest of the day. Eventually our conversations most always steered toward the Five Finger Mountains and what we experienced up there.

One year passed after the war ended before I visited Charleston, the capital of our new state. I found the address of Captain Patton's wife and children through the local post office and stopped by unannounced to express my heartfelt condolences. He, above all others, showed me what it was like to be utterly courageous while staring at certain defeat.

Not many people remained in Cucumber after the war. Moss and I would take on odd jobs here and there to make a little money, but really, we mostly had more than enough. After all, Moss knew how to tend to the land, and had learned to plant corn, tomatoes, lettuce, and beets.

"As a free man, I need to tend to my own garden before complaining about some ones else's weeds," he would say, vigorously tilling the dirt.

We each had parts and duties to perform for our small collective. Each one of us pitching in. But August and I took a different path than Moss. We were damaged goods. Two broken vessels.

For Moss, it was over.

But for me and August… it was vengeance.

Every so often, together, August and I would take a day trip over to the library in Beckleyville. We not only searched for her uncle and cousin (whom we never found) but we also craved to understand what happened on top of that bloody mountain. There were times we also traveled overnight to the Seminary School located in Shepherdstown to study writings and texts in an attempt to understand. Try to make sense of what happened to us.

We tried to heal as best we could, but there are some scars you can't see and that never heal. Every now and then, Moss would catch us sitting by the graves. He would join us there and we would wonder aloud about that strange, horrible time upon the mountain.

He would then walk back into the home of my father… and seem to be at peace.

But not August…and especially not me. And no one is more dangerous than a man who can't lock down his own emotions.

Five Years Later...

CHAPTER 39

Thurmond

Thurmond, West Virginia

The town of Thurmond was located in the newly-formed state of West Virginia, and it was a virtual shithole of a place. The post office was built by Captain W.D. Thurmond in 1866 and, due to its location along the Chesapeake & Ohio Rail Line and the New River, the town immediately exploded in growth.

Especially the red-light district known as "The Ballyhack."

Every night, coal miners, railroaders, loggers, tie walkers, and river boaters converged on The Ballyhack. Thurmond was the Dodge City of the east and The Ballyhack's average death rate was four or five men a night, every night. If you had the money in your pocket, you could buy whisky, moonshine, women, men, and any other thing a man could imagine... if the price was right. There were opium dens nestled beside brothels alongside saloons, dance halls, and sleeping taverns, all for the taking.

And the man who owned it all was none other than Colonel Jacob 'Black Damp' McCabe.

Black Damp insisted that he be called Colonel, and he was as ruthless in business as he was in war. He made his fortune in both suffering and hopelessness, and he showed it by building a massive colonial mansion on top of the largest hill overlooking the town.

Like a typical southern estate, the front porch was large and expansive. Its gaudiness was as audacious as a garter belt was to a whore. The second floor boasted another large, wraparound porch which mirrored the lower level. There, off Black Damp's bedroom, he could view the cesspool that he helped create.

The estate featured mosaic crown molding, inlaid with turquois stones which bestowed good fortune on all who entered. The roof was enclosed by glass, covering a sizeable ballroom with marble tile flooring imported from Spain. The first floor contained several butler kitchens and a large dining room which could sit at least 20 guests.

It would have been magnificent and breathtaking, if not for the evil living inside.

Thurmond's main inn was known as the Dun Glen, or "Dunglen," as the locals would call her. She featured Cabaret shows, gambling halls, and underground shops. It was once dubbed the "Waldorf of the Mountains," and true to her name, the 100-room luxury hotel boasted a wraparound verandah taking advantage of the prestigious and panoramic mountain vistas and views of the New River. She was the only diamond in a town full of rust.

At around midnight under an insipid moon a couple weeks before All-Hallows E'en, three riders approached the town of Thurmond. About a mile before reaching the town's boundary, they stopped. Two of the riders were dressed in all black, and both were heavily armed. Each carried two pistols, one tucked into a side holster and the other in a hidden holster around the back of the waist. Both riders also had Bowie knives, tied to sheaths along their boots. They were as sharp as the finest razors. The third rider drove a wagon. She carried a small derringer tucked under her corset as well as another small pistol and a long, straight-edged knife in a secret side pocket.

As they stopped, the riders spoke softly to one another before one led his horse about 30 yards into the woods, tethering it to a large willow. If anybody glanced over from the road, the weeping willow branches hid the horse well. The rider who dismounted nodded to the other two and disappeared into a heavily wooded area south of town.

The remaining two slowly rode into town, passing all the revelry, crowds, and townsfolk who would occasionally spill out onto the main dirt road which weaved through the center of town.

No one noticed as they both rode into The Ballyhack and past the Dun Glen Hotel, circling behind the massive structure to stop in a small alleyway located to the left of the inn. The rider in black got off his horse, scanning around to see if anyone was watching. Meanwhile, the woman jumped down from the wagon, smoothed her dress, and sprayed herself (for the third time that night) with French Acqua Rosa perfume.

Standing under a soft streetlight, the woman's Southern Belle red gown shimmered in the glow, and her painted red nails and ruby lips gave an air of mystery and desire. She swayed her hips as she flashed a black garter belt wrapped around her left thigh. Her long black hair ran down her shoulders in ringlets to the middle of her breasts, accentuated with a tight corset.

She was a stunner.

Putting away the perfume, she looked at the third man standing in the shadows and batted her eyelashes with a sly smile. "Why hello, big boy. You looken for a good time?"

The man in the shadows gave a deep laugh and replied, "Why, yes ma'am, I sure am. But let's take care of business before we start something that we can't finish."

The woman laughed and casually flipped her hair off to the side. "Why, are you sure you can handle this southern belle?"

"Oh, yeah. I'll be able to handle her," the man said with a grin, addressing the woman from top to bottom. "Now remember, I'll follow you in after about five minutes. Don't look for me. I'll be there when the time's right."

For the first time, the woman showed a hint of hesitation. "I know... I know... but don't leave my ass hangin' in the wind."

Facing one another, the woman in red reached up with her right hand and slowly caressed a jagged scar which ran down the man's cheek to his chin.

"That scar has healed up right nice," she said softly. "Makes you look... fierce."

The man laughed and gave her a quick hug. He leaned in to kiss her but she batted him away. "Not on the lips."

That's exactly what the man wanted but instead he kissed her on the cheek.

ঙ

As she entered the rear door, the man in black was able to hear the loud music from inside. *Good*, he thought, *that will make this whole thing much easier.*

He walked around to the front of the inn and saw several people sitting in chairs along the wide-covered porch. Not one looked his way. He breathed deep and then entered two large swinging doors into a massive room. On the far side stood a small stage where several girls danced and swayed with one another, dressed in sailor's uniforms. To the left was a large bar with three bartenders serving drinks to about 10 to 12 patrons.

There were several cages throughout the room, with a woman in each cage. None were fully dressed.

Along the right side of the room were three or four card tables with men and women playing poker or the dealer's card game of choice. Within a few seconds, the man in black approximated the number of people at the bar, Cabaret, and gambling tables and figured it was well over 100.

Remaining hidden in the smoky shadows, he walked over to the nearest bartender and ordered a whiskey, straight up. As the bartender poured the whiskey into a glass, he leaned over and whispered into the bartender's ear. The bartender nodded and pointed over to the farthest poker table. The man smiled and tossed back the whiskey with one gulp. The bartender poured him another and then exited the bar, walking over to the table where several men were playing.

All at once, he felt a light touch on my shoulder and a voice whispered into his opposite ear. "Why hello, sugar." He turned slightly to face the voice.

And there, staring into his face, was Sarah.

ஒ

Sarah. The girl of my childhood dreams. *My God,* I thought.

I hadn't prepared for this.

She leaned in tight to my ear and whispered, "Let me be your sweet peach tonight." I immediately turned my head back to the bartender so she couldn't get a good look at my face.

"Honey, you wanna go?" she said, this time more forcibly. She then placed her hand on my crotch and began to run her hand up and down.

It was obvious that she was drunk. It was also obvious that she was not the same little girl from class that I remembered.

She was very thin and pale, dark makeup applied way too thick and sloppy. Her smudged mascara made what was once alert and dazzling eyes into soulless pits. She sported a large bruise, which she attempted to cover up with makeup, on her right cheek.

"No miss, but thank you, nonetheless," I said, pushing her hand away and meeting her gaze.

For a moment, I saw her hesitate. A brief form of recognition. Swaying on her feet, she cocked her head sideways and squinted. "Don't I know you from somewhere? Were you the young man that…?"

"No miss, that wasn't me," I said quickly before turning away. Sarah looked me up and down and turned away, mumbling, "Suit yourself, but you're missin' one hell of a good time."

As I watched her leave, she flipped around and blew a kiss before melting into the crowd. I felt a wave of pity for her. But as quickly as it came, I shoved it back down, having hardened my heart a long time ago.

War and death does that sometimes.

I turned back to my spot at the bar and several minutes later the bartender approached and whispered in my ear. "You're up."

Pulling out a wad of bills, I placed them on the table and muttered, "It's all yours," before weaving myself in and out of the crowd to the farthest poker table at the wall.

There sat several men, and the one who sat at the opposite of the only vacant chair at the table was Colonel Black Damp McCabe.

As I sat down, he glanced up and was met with an icy cold stare. "And who might you be... boy?" he said in a loud, booming voice so those nearby could hear. Hearing no response, he mumbled to himself, "Southern trash."

"Whom," I said coolly.

"What?" replied Black Damp, narrowing his eyes. "What did you say?"

"Whom," I repeated. "It's whom might you be?"

We each stared at one another, neither saying a word.

The man to the left started dealing out the cards. "Five Card Stud, deuces wild. The bet is 10 dollars to play."

The Colonel was playing well tonight. He had a deep stack. But I had no intention of playing this card game past a round or two.

I had many more important things on my mind this night.

As I put 20 dollars into the kitty, the dealer dealt five cards. I looked down at my hand and saw three aces, an eight of spades, and a Jack of Hearts. I glanced up and saw the Colonel staring directly at me.

"I'm out," the dealer announced, placing his cards on the table.

"Me too," replied the man to the right of the Colonel.

"It's just you and me... boy,'" he said with a sneer.

I stared at my cards, then reached into my pockets and produced a 50-dollar bill. I then put it in the middle of the table.

Staring at me, Black Damp furrowed his brow. "I've seen your face before."

I stared back into his soulless eyes. Black Damp then slid a matching 50 out into the middle of the table.

"I call," he said, not taking his eyes off me.

We laid our cards on the table. Black Damp produced a king of spades, queen of hearts, a four and three of diamonds, and a seven of clubs.

"Fuck me," said the Colonel as he leaned back in his chair. It was his first poor hand.

As I reached over to collect the winnings, Sarah appeared out of nowhere. She stared intently at me for a moment before leaning down and whispering into the Colonel's ear. Black Damp McCabe then smiled.

The Colonel rose up from his chair and stretched his arms out wide. "Gentleman, if you will excuse me, I have another engagement upstairs that needs tending to," he said, grabbing at his crotch. He then glanced over at me and winked. "Darlin', would you be my dixie cup and cash in these chips?" he said to Sarah before turning and heading toward the stairs.

All the men within earshot started laughing and jeering at one another. Except me. I, too, slowly rose from the table and stuffed the money into my pocket. Sarah floated away, disappearing into the crowd and smoke.

The music died down as the Cabaret show ended. I slunk back once more and made my way over to the same stairs that Black Damp had taken. If Sarah had recognized me, there was nothing much that I could do about it now.

The plan so carefully laid out a year ago was still on…or so I thought.

CHAPTER 40
Upstairs

When August first entered the Dun Glen, she was immediately met by Sarah waiting for her at the bar's entrance.

"Right on time, honey," she said, flashing a smile. Several of her side teeth were missing along the left side of her face exposing a gaping hole when she smiled. She asked August to turn around and gave her a cursory once-over.

"He's gonna like you. That's for sure,'" she said, licking her lips and taking another drink.

August smiled and said in her best Southern drawl, "Why, thank you miss…er, pardon my manners, but what was your name again?"

Sarah lit up a cigarette and blew the smoke directly at her. "Sarah. But never you mind. Go on upstairs, it's the last door on your left." As August turned and began to head up the stairs, Sarah continued. "Now, you've done this sort of thing before, right?"

Stopping in the middle of the stairs, August replied without turning around. "Why yes, er… yes, I have. Many times, in fact. Why, just the other day…"

"Save it," Sarah said, interrupting her. "Don't forget…he likes it rough. Real rough." And with that, Sarah was gone, making the rounds and greeting the newly arriving customers entering the hotel.

As August continued up the stairs, she kept up the performance. She entered the second floor, knowing full well that all the rooms would be on her left. We had scouted and prepared for this night years ago. The view from the balcony on the right had a commanding view of the lower-level gambling hall and Cabaret. We both knew where the other one was at all times. I could look up to the second floor and she could look down, keeping us connected and on schedule.

She lingered a little, slowly making her way down the hall to the last door on the left. She looked around to see if anyone was watching and then opened the door and walked in.

She turned on a small gas lamp on a nightstand beside a large bed, and went over to a window overlooking a rear alley and fire escape. She quietly unlocked the window.

She took in her surroundings. The bed was enormous, with a thick wooden headboard and bedposts. On the nightstand was a photograph of Colonel Black Damp in his uniform and a heavy cannonball paperweight. There was a large wooden desk near the left side of the wall with papers scattered on it, and behind that were two large French doors leading out to a veranda. She could see lower main street and of the New River beyond, and about a quarter of a mile away, the Colonel's sprawling mansion.

August reached in her purse and took out her perfume, nervously spraying the room. She also pulled out a second small derringer, placing it underneath one of the pillows on the bed.

Just as she finished fluffing the pillow, the door opened, and Black Damp McCabe entered.

He stopped in the doorway and stared at her. He flashed a crooked smile before shutting the door and slowly taking off his coat, letting it drop to the floor.

August swallowed. "Why, sir, you need to pick that up before it gets soiled and all."

He smirked, not taking his eyes off her. "Cut the crap and kneel down."

She did as she was told.

Black Damp began to remove his belt from his pants. August looked up at him and batted her eyes. "Why, let me help with that." She reached up and with her right hand slowly caressed his leg and inner thigh.

He closed his eyes, muttering, "Goddamn. You're gonna make me a lot of money."

He opened his eyes as she slowly stood up. August drew his head close to hers, their lips within inches of one another. She slowly licked her lips and said, "It be more comfortable on the bed. I like it rough....and dirty....and the bed makes it more comfortable that way."

"Way ahead of ya, darlin'," he replied. She could feel his excitement. He hurriedly stripped off his shirt and pants. He sat down on the bed to take off his socks when she pushed him back on the bed.

August positioned her head between Black Damp's legs and looked up at him with a smile. "Sugar, why don't you just keep them on for a while?"

He closed his eyes, anticipating her touch. However, she slowly got up from her knees and helped him stand up from the bed.

"Turn around, love. This is a little trick I learned in Thailand."

He did as he was told, and as she bent him over, she reached for the cannonball paperweight. With all her might, August drew the projectile back and slammed it on the back side of his head. With a grunt, he collapsed on the floor.

Breathing heavy, she laid the cannonball on the bed and stood up.

"Thailand? Really?"

Turning, she looked at me. I stepped into the room and shut the door.

"A woman is allowed to improvise from time to time," she replied with a wink. "Hurry, help me carry him to the rug by the window and we'll wrap him up."

I quickly rushed where Black Damp had fallen, grabbing his feet while August lifted his shoulders. We hoisted him up and carried him over to a small carpet, which was laying by window nearest to the fire escape. I checked to make sure that he was breathing, then we rolled him up with only his feet and face exposed. August grabbed a small handkerchief from her purse and stuffed it into his mouth.

"On the count of three, we lift him up and out the window. The son of a bitch will fall onto the veranda floor and then…."

A voice rang out from the doorway. "He may be a son of a bitch…but he's MY son of a bitch."

I whipped around.

Sarah.

She held small pistol in her right hand, aimed directly at me.

"Well now. Greasy Reecy… it took me awhile, but I finally recognized you," she said, looking me over. "My… you've changed. Looks like the war all done caught up with you."

August scowled and snapped, "Look who's talking."

"Shut up, bitch," Sarah hissed, leveling her eyes at August. She let out a raspy laugh. "Why Reece, if I'd known it was you, I would have done you for free." She batted her eyes at me before turning to look at August. "You see, honey, Reece and I go way back… don't we, darlin'?"

August narrowed her eyes as her face flushed. Sarah continued. "You see your boyfriend here has a little crush on me. Isn't that right… my little Reece?"

"You mean *had* one," I snapped, more defensively that I intended.

Sarah looked at August and then at me. She took a step closer to me, keeping the gun raised. "I could make you forget her. I could take you and show you what a real woman's like," she said in a drawl, slightly biting her lower lip.

August took a step closer to Sarah and scowled. "Touch him and I'll rip the bark right off you."

Sarah spun to face August, leveling her pistol at August's head. "Take one more step, and I'll blow your fuckin' head off. Now, unwrap him and set him on the bed," she said, motioning towards the limp body by the window. "NOW!"

August and I turned toward the window when we first caught sight of the flames outside. Sarah screamed and rushed towards the window facing Main Street.

"NO… oh my God, no! NO!" she wailed. But before she reached the window, I grabbed the cannonball from the bed and smashed her on the left side of her face.

She dropped immediately to the floor next to Black Damp. Out cold.

I looked at August and she looked at me, as the sky lit up the outside walls of the Dun Glen in a blaze of red and orange.

CHAPTER 41

Our Escape

We stood there in the middle of the room, looking at the two bodies lying on the floor and listening to the yelling and commotion coming from the outside. Peering down from the second floor of the Dun Glen Motel, we could see that the mansion up on the hill – Black Damp's prized possession, looming over the entire town of Thurmond – was engulfed in flames.

Orange flames spilled out of every window, the oversized front doors, and even from the top of the estate's three chimneys.

I spun around and grabbed August's arm. "Right on cue," I said with a grin.

We wrapped Sarah in a bed sheet and, one at a time, carried each out of the window and set them on the veranda. I then jumped down onto the wagon bed from the second story room and August gently rolled Black Damp down to me. I placed him in the wagon bed first. She then took the limp body of Sarah and – without waiting for me – rolled her off the veranda, where she roughly landed on the Colonel's body.

Under her breath, August muttered, "Bitch."

So far, no one noticed. People spilled into the streets, and everyone's eyes were on the fire. Black Damp McCabe's fire.

August then lowered herself down on to the wagon where I was able to grab her legs and pull her into my arms.

Shaking her head, she quickly kissed my cheek before pushing me away. "THAT was your girlfriend? You had a crush on THAT?"

I smiled. "We don't really have time for this now, considering the whole town is about 40 feet away," I replied. "And she WASN'T my girlfriend." As we lowered ourselves into the wagon carriage, Black Damp opened his eyes and groaned.

"Shut up!" snapped August before grabbing his head and smacking it against the back of the wooden box seat. He became still.

I honestly thought she had killed him.

We spurred the horses out of the alley and on to Main Street. We were met with pure pandemonium. Everyone was screaming and running this way and that. No one noticed as a wagon slowly paraded down Main Street in the middle of the madness.

The street was vacant when we approached the end of town. This section of the road was the closest to the river, and the fire at the mansion produced an eerie glow, blanketing the entire area. As we rode alongside the river, I caught sight of motion coming from behind. As I glanced back around, I saw Sarah leap from the wagon bed and on to the dirt road, her head bloody from where August hit her.

I immediately jumped down from my horse and yelled for August to stop. Sarah scrambled up, trying to make a run for it. Realizing I was quicker, she grabbed a stick on the side of the road and leveled the branch toward me.

"Don't come any closer!" she screamed. "Don't come any closer!"

"Sarah… Sarah… drop the stick. We didn't come for you. We came for him," I said evenly, pointing to the wagon.

She laughed. "I know why you're here. But you're wrong. Don't you see? You're so stupid! You and your Pa. Country bumkins. IT WAS ME! It was ME that led him to the dance that night! ME!"

I stood there in shock. I didn't know what to say. "Sarah… why?"

MY FAMILY AND I HATED YOU! I HATED BOTH OF YOU! YOUR 'HOLIER THAN THOU' CONFEDERACY. ALL OF IT! WE SHOWED YOU ALL!" she screamed wildly.

She started swinging the stick back and forth, crying and laughing at the same time as she backed away. Neither of us saw the large rock, covered by grass, lying beside the road.

Sarah backed up further. "Stay away!" she shrieked.

I kept my voice steady. "Sarah… don't take another step. You're gonna trip and fall into the river."

She just laughed and then took another step backward. Her left foot caught the top of the rock, and she tumbled backwards and over the bank of the river.

The New River. The Indians call it the *Great Kahnaway* or *The River of Death.*

I rushed over to where she fell and looked down. Sarah

231

clung to a small root sticking out from the mud of the river bank with one hand. She thrashed wildly sideways in the whitewater, its current trying to drag her both downward and outward towards the jagged rocks a few feet away.

"REECE! REECE! Help me! Help me! I can't swim!" she screamed, her eyes pleading with me.

"SARAH!" I yelled. I grabbed the stick that she dropped on the ground and lowered it to her. "Grab the stick!" I yelled. "Here! Grab the stick and I will pull you up!"

Her head went under water and then popped back up. "I... can't... sw...." she gurgled. She went under again.

Suddenly, Moss appeared at my side. August jumped out of the wagon and rushed over. "Her dress... HER DRESS!" August yelled over the noise of the river. "IT'S DRAGGING HER DOWN!"

Sarah's head bobbed up for the last time – and then it was over. She just stopped yelling and screaming and simply let go. Her eyes locked on mine as she was swept away by the rapids that this river is known for. And then her head went under, and she never resurfaced. As the spring rain gave way to the summer heat, they found her body about five miles downstream eight months later.

I stood there, not knowing what to think. Why would she do that to me? To my father? To Boone and Caleb?

I didn't understand. And to this day, I still don't know what really happened to Sarah. What demons she had hidden deep within her soul.

Turning, I looked at Moss. In a daze, I said softly. "She was in it with him. Goddamnit, she was in with him."

August led me to the wagon and horses. No one spoke except for Moss, who muttered quietly, "Let's go."

And so we did.

We rode until the break of dawn and pulled over to a prearranged spot. It was about 50 feet from the main road over a small knoll that no one traveling could see. We changed clothes, made a small fire, and rested from the night's events.

Black Damp slipped in and out of consciousness a few times throughout the night and morning hours. Each time he tried to speak, August would look over at him and take out her knife. Finally, she stuck a bandana in his mouth.

Around midday the next day, Moss sat down next to me as I rested next to the fire. "We got to feed him? Don't you think?"

"Where he's going, I don't think it matters," I replied. "Go ahead and give him something, but don't take off his bindings."

Moss pulled out the handkerchief that August had stuck in his mouth.

Colonel Jacob "Black Damp" McCabe gasped and coughed before turning his head towards me. At that moment, I saw the glimmer of recognition.

"You," he muttered in a raspy breath. "You… I remember you! You're that squirrely kid years ago. You took a shot at me and then ran away…. on the Droop. I know who you are."

"What else?" I said coolly, staring straight at him.

"What do you mean what else?" he scoffed. I could see a faint glint of fear in his eyes.

August walked up and handed me a cup of coffee. "You heard him," she hissed, turning toward him.

I stood, walking over and kneeling down in front of him. "What else?" I repeated, trying with everything I had to keep my voice steady.

Black Damp just sat there, eyes darting from me to August and back again. There was no acknowledgement from him about what he did to my father.

Nothing. He didn't even remember.

"Tell you what," I said, getting back up, and losing my composure. "I'll give you a hint. You took from me everything! EVERYTHING! You took from me the one thing in my life that mattered the most!"

"What... who?" he replied, staring up at us.

I stepped back, my hands shaking. I took a deep breath and felt August's hand on my back. I looked over at her, our eyes locking for a moment. She reached up and touched my cheek before turning back to Black Damp, kicking him squarely in the ribs.

"Think hard about it, and maybe then we'll give you some water and food," she said, narrowing her eyes at him.

Black Damp said nothing for a long time after that, his eyes darting around, always following me. I think he was honestly trying to remember.

It was late in the day when we broke camp. Moss doused the fire while August and I policed the area, making sure that no one would ever know that we were there. As darkness fell, we loaded up and proceeded on.

After all... we had a schedule to keep.

CHAPTER 42

Revenge

It took us two days to reach the midpoint of our journey, and another day to reach the bottom of The Five Finger Mountains. Midway, we camped overnight at Sam Black Church. I found myself flooded with memories when the cart rolled to a stop in front of the old, burned out building. Memories of Boone, Caleb, Pa... of a life that felt so long ago. We rested and decided to give the Colonel something to eat and drink.

He tried at this point to become an associate, a compatriot. We would have none of it.

He started rambling as he ate. He wouldn't shut up. Black Damp McCabe insisted that he was religious man now. A man of God. It was necessary, he said, for all of us to act according to "God's Will."

"After all," he pleaded, "*Thou shall not kill.*"

August and I remained quiet. The only words directed at him were from Moss. "The Word of God teaches us that thou shall not murder. And you call yourself a religious man?" he said quietly, shaking his head. He did not wait for an answer. "For what you've done, for all you have murdered and injured in YOUR name, where you're going…you're gonna need some God."

We once again broke camp the next morning, keeping a relentless pace. We briefly stopped at the tree where Jed was killed. It had been eight years since he was murdered, and five years since the war ended. I hoped that this would jog Black Damp's memory. If it did, the Colonel didn't show it. He just sat in the wagon and stared at the three of us.

We arrived at the bottom of the Five Finger Mountains at – exactly – the same date and time as when I arrived those many years ago.

But August and I had done our homework since that day. After the war, we studied and we learned. We delved into old religious teachings, describing what I stumbled onto on that horrific night. We wrote letters to authorities, people who specialized in such things.

And exactly one year ago on this date, August and I traveled to the top of the cursed mountain to lay the second engraved headstones I had crafted to place there in their memory. There, we witnessed once again the blasphemous hole… in all its wonder.

And it was there that she and I started making the plans that led us to now.

Under a bright, full moon, we finally set up camp at the bottom of the third mountain. Black Damp had now become very quiet; in fact, none of us spoke much. In the distance, we could hear the howl of wolves.

No one slept peacefully that night.

Early in the morning, we awoke and began to prepare for our climb. We left most of our provisions at the base of the mountain, making sure that the horses were well-fed and that both they and the wagon were hidden from sight.

Before starting our climb, we untied the bindings that restrained Black Damp's legs. He started laughing and shook his head from side to side. "I'm not going up there," he said with a confident smirk on his face. "You can't make me."

August looked at me and then at Moss. "Did he say that we couldn't make him go up this mountain? Is that what he said?"

"Yes ma'am, that's exactly what he said," replied Moss in a soft voice, glancing up at the mountain. Knowing something about retribution himself, he did not smile.

He understood what we were doing and what it meant.

August glanced over at me, and I gave her a slight nod in agreement. She then went to her saddlebag and took out a very large, very sharp set of wire cutters. She showed it to Black Damp with a dangerous and dark grin on her face. "Oh, you're going up there, with or without..." she trailed off, and looked down at his crotch.

He scowled at her, but didn't say another word until we arrived on top of the mountain.

It took us a full day of climbing, taking a couple of breaks around noon and three. The higher we climbed the middle mountain, the more obvious it became that the upper portions of the mountain had...*changed*. It had become even more desolate and felt more isolated than the rest of the mountain below. It was autumn; however, there were no fallen leaves to be found. It appeared that the trees had been dead for quite some time – more rotten than what I remembered, even since last year's journey. There was an overwhelming stench of decay. Where shrubs and grass once grew, there was only dirt and rock.

God's sunlight rarely reveals itself to the unholy.

Black Damp became more agitated. Finally, during our rest in the late afternoon, he looked at me and asked quietly, "What are you going to do to me?"

I did not say a thing. I left him to stew, to think about all that he had done in his pitiful life.

We finally reached the top of the mountain by early evening and located our spot where we camped years ago. There was still enough light to gather firewood, and as we began to search around, we discovered our old lean-to which we made on the second night all those years before. Most of the sticks used for the roof had either broken or blown away. It was just a lump of brush in the forest now. The gravestones lay where they were placed, not having moved an inch.

Moss lit a fire and began to prepare a stew. The same supper we had hours before the creature attacked on that fateful night.

Before we sat down to eat, August and I walked through the woods, moving together side by side, not saying a word as we hiked through the barren trees, searching for that spot.

The place where the beast had stolen our family.

We stepped out of the woods and there it was, in all its glory and horror. The massive pit, ready to swallow up anything that entered. I had forgotten how large the opening truly was, and as I stared at it, frozen to the spot, the memories flooded back. One year ago, we witnessed the shock of its opening. At that time, we did not linger. Our mission had been completed by laying the second set of headstones. Gravesites without bodies to lay to rest, without truly knowing what had become of the people taken to the depths below.

August took my hand and held it in hers. Without looking at me, she said softly, mostly to herself, "Do you think they're still alive?"

"I guess we'll see," I replied, gently squeezing her hand.

I wanted to believe. I wanted to think that somehow, someway, they were there. Alive, and waiting for us. I wanted to hold on tight to that hope, as much for August's sake as for my own.

But in my heart, I knew the truth.

We stood there, hand in hand, rooted to the spot. Finally, we turned around and returned to our base camp. Moss had finished preparing the stew and we sat down by the fire to eat. The Colonel sat next to Moss, his face illuminated by the orange flames in the darkness that had fallen over our little camp. His eyes darted back and forth, and he barely ate a bite. I watched as the panic began to etch itself across his face, and he shivered in the cool night breeze despite the warmth of the fire.

I kept my face blank, emotionless, as I spoke to him.

"In the morning, here's what's going to happen. We are going to get up, pack some supplies, and continue our journey down into a cavern."

"Are you going to kill me then?" he hissed, smirking despite the obvious fear in his eyes. "Why don't you get on with it and just throw me off one of these ledges scattered around here and be done with it!"

I looked him directly in the eyes, matching his ice-cold stare. "No. WE are not going to kill you. You are going to be judged."

"Judged? By who?" he scoffed, glancing over at August, who was listening intently to every word.

"Whom." I replied. "By whom."

He fell silent. There was no more conversation for the rest of the night.

ᐔ

Moss, August, and Black Damp bedded in for the night. We retied the Colonel's leg restraints, and I made sure that the fire was stoked and kept first watch.

It was eerily quiet outside, and I did not hear a sound coming from the surrounding woods that whole night. The full moon provided ample light to see any nearby movement in the trees. I saw nothing during the hours of my watch. August relieved me around two in the morning, as she could not sleep. We decided to let Moss sleep – the only one of us all who was able to get some much-needed rest. The Colonel was wide awake all night, wondering or planning…who knows which.

Right on schedule, we rose at the break of dawn. While I prepared breakfast, August and Moss packed for the journey ahead.

We brought along a few surprises. We each carried two lanterns with extra filament and oil stored in our shoulder bags, along with liniment ointment, wraps, and splints… just in case. We also had the pistols and knives we carried with us when we took the Colonel, as well as three, double-barreled, sawed-off shotguns.

We were as prepared as we could possibly be for what lie ahead.

I took out my knife as we trekked slowly through the woods, finally breaking through the forest to reach the clearing. I saddled up to the Colonel, who backed away once he saw my weapon. Moss grabbed ahold of him and held him still so I could cut his leg bindings allowing his feet to move freely. I made sure that both of his hands remained tied tight in front of his body.

As we approached the brim of the pit, he stopped cold, jaw dropping as he looked down.

"Jesus Christ," he gasped. He paused a moment, staring down with his mouth wide open. His eyes widened in shock as he turned to me. "My God, what is this?"

I was about to reply *your tomb* but I decided to say nothing and shoved him forward.

And down we went.

We lit the lanterns on top and with all three aglow, it was easy to follow the granite stairs down. Every so often, we would stop to rest and take a drink from our canteens.

I looked up after a long time, and could not see the entrance to the cavern. And soon, August stopped and said quietly, "There it is."

Barely, just barely, we could see the glow of the small fire.

We doused all but one lantern to conserve our fuel and proceeded down further. Black Damp turned back to look at August, his eyes shining with excitement. It was as if the wonder of this place overtook his fear and he flashed a wide smile. "My GOD! What have you discovered? This is amazing! Truly a find of the century! This must be reported. Why, people would pay a small fortune to see this! You MUST let me go. We can all be rich together!"

"Shut up," I said sharply in response. "Keep going."

We finally reached the bottom. It was nearly the same as when we escaped years ago. There were no footprints in the sand, no cut bindings around the post.

It was as if no one had ever been there.

I stepped carefully down onto the smooth floor, my eyes darting back and forth to look for any signs of the creatures. The Colonel stopped on the last stair step. He paused for only a moment, looking around, before jumping down and pushing ahead of me. "We must explore this place! There could be hidden gold or jewels!" he said, turning around wildly to scan the area. He begged me to cut his bindings, promising that all of us could search together. He promised that he would not try to escape.

Walking towards him, I pulled out my knife. Smiling, I cut the bindings that tied his hands in front.

"Thank God, boy, you've come to your senses!" he laughed maniacally, rubbing his wrists with his hands.

But his freedom was brief. Moss and I quickly grabbed ahold of him tightly, seizing his arms. We led him over to the post in the center of the space, pulling both his arms behind his back while August tied his hands back together.

"UNTIE ME! YOU FOOLS!' he screamed, his eyes wide with surprise and anger. "DON'T ANY OF YOU UNDERSTAND?"

After securing his hands again, August moved to face him and slapped him hard across the face. "Shut up and be quiet!"

He turned his head to look at me, silently pleading. I took a step closer until I was inches away from him. I spoke in a low voice, trying to keep steady and calm, but the rage I had been holding back was beginning to take shape.

"Eight years ago, you… YOU… entered my life. You don't remember, but I do," I said as I tried to keep as my voice from quivering. "How could I forget? I was only 14 when you took the person that meant the most to me. A person that was kind and generous… my father. You drove a two-foot sword through his belly so deep that only the breastbone stopped the hilt."

I paused for a moment, the memory of that day swirling in my mind. I lowered my head and closed my eyes. "He had never done an evil thing to anybody… let alone to you! But you took his life right before my eyes, and I have never – never – forgotten you, or what you did."

I looked up at Colonel "Black Damp" McCabe. I could see him, dimly in the faint glow of the flames from the fire, and at that moment, that very moment, I could tell that he knew. He knew of my father's death by his hand. He knew that all his sins, all his wickedness had now finally caught up with him.

Suddenly, his eyes opened wide, as if he saw a ghost. He focused his stare behind August and began to whimper softly. I followed his gaze, gripping my shotgun tightly.

The door, the small door which we had passed through eight years before, was slowly opening.

I raised my shotgun at the open door, sliding quickly over to the side and pointing it at the opening.

But nothing came out.

August and Moss took positions directly opposite of the door. They, too, pointed their weapons at the opening. After what seemed like an eternity, I took our small lantern and carefully bent down and stuck it about a foot inside the doorway.

Nothing. Nothing at all.

Bewildered, I turned around to look at August and Moss. They both knelt down and peered into the entrance.

Nothing.

I reached in and with the end of the shotgun pushed the lantern further inside. It was so quiet, I felt like everyone could hear my heart beating wildly in my chest. The glow from the lantern illuminated a little further, and I could see something outlined on the ground. I leaned in slightly, squinting and craning my neck to get a view.

There, along the edge of the light just barely visible, was the Major's journal. It looked to be in the same condition as when I last saw it in the Major's hands, unaffected and untarnished by the many years that have passed.

I couldn't believe my eyes.

"AUGUST! AUGUST! Your father's journal!" I whispered loudly, motioning for her to come closer. She edged forward, dropping her shotgun and kneeling down behind me.

I turned to meet her eyes. "This may contain all the answers." I reached forward to grab the journal, but August yanked at my arm, pulling it back. I looked back at her, but she was looking straight ahead, her eyes wide.

"Shhhhhhh," she said, so softly I could barely hear her. She placed a finger alongside her lips. "Darling… don't make another move. Look behind the book along the right side of the wall. Do you see it?"

I followed her gaze and looked past the journal. There, at the edge of the light, I could just make out the very tip of a long claw. It shook, ever so slightly, in anticipation, like a cat waiting to pounce upon a mouse.

My chest felt tight, and I could feel the blood pulsing through my veins. *I can do it*, I thought, *I can do it*!

I looked at August, so beautiful in the light of the lantern. I felt my love for her tighten, even as fear gripped me. I HAD to find out what happened to her father – for her. That desire was just as strong as my need to find out what happened to Boone and Caleb.

'No," I whispered softly, turning my eyes away from hers. "I need to know.'" But as I turned around to reach into the doorway, it appeared that the decision was not mine to make. At that moment, the creature stepped out into the light, its sharp teeth smiling and drool running down its mouth.

Startled, I fell backwards into August, and we both collapsed onto the sandy floor. We both backpedaled toward Moss. The creature, like a spider dropping from its web, slowly emerged from the doorway.

"Scare it away! Give us some time to escape!" I screamed at Moss, who fumbled with his shotgun. "SHOOT IT!"

Moss raced over and pointed the gun directly at the creature's head and fired. The head splintered into two pieces, like a lightning bolt splitting down the center of a tree – both pieces still attached to its body. Moss had cleaved the head directly in two.

Then, as we sat there in stunned silence, we watched both pieces come back together.

"MOTHER OF GOD!" Black Damp shrieked. I had almost forgotten he was there. "MOTHER OF GOD! SWEET JESUS, UNTIE ME!"

I scrambled to my feet, grabbing August by the back of her coat and yanking her up. The shotgun sounded again, deafening in the small space. My ears began to ring.

I screamed at August and Moss. "GO! GO NOW!"

As they raced towards the stairs, I turned to face the creature and fired round after round into its body. That seemed to stop its momentum for a few moments, giving me enough time to also head for the stairs. As my feet touched the first step, August grabbed me by the collar, pulling me up the stairs towards her. Moss fumbled to light our second lantern ahead of her as we raced up the stairs. I looked down and saw the beast slowly turn to Colonel "Black Damp" McCabe.

The beast, as if a peacock, reared itself up in all its splendor. Black Damp furiously struggled against his bindings, trying to escape, shaking the pole back and forth.

But my bindings held fast.

With one step forward, the creature was suddenly standing beside him, staring down. It could have easily picked up him and the pole together in one fell swoop.

But it had other ideas.

The demon opened its mouth wide, displaying its razor-sharp teeth. I watched as Black Damp looked up, still flaying around in terror.

He then stopped struggling.

With its jaws open wide, the beast slowly lowered its mouth over Black Damp's head down to his chest and clamped its teeth. Slowly, ever so slowly, it began to draw its mouth upward, raking its teeth over his chest and head.

When he rose back up, Black Damp's body was unrecognizable, clothes and skin in tatters. With blood, bone and tendons dripping off its teeth, the creature then turned and stared up at me.

I realized I had stopped running, stopped my climb. I stood there in disbelief. The horror of what we had just witnessed rendered us all frozen, rooted to the spot on the stairs. It was even more brutal than I could have ever imagined.

It was Moss who noticed the other creatures. The ones with the red eyes. Its legions.

They were now starting to come out of the doorway.

"GO! GO NOW!" he yelled, his voice strained from what we had just witnessed. August again yanked hard upon my collar, and as if snapping me out of a trance, I turned and we resumed running up the stairs as fast as we could.

The small creatures poured out of the doorway, snarling and scraping their claws against the sand floor.

Our route was straight up the stairs, same as before. The third time now that I had run up those stairs, fleeing for my life from the horrors below. The creatures, with their sharp claws, could maneuver along the sides of the walls and on the sides of the stairs.

They quickly started to outflank us.

Moss was brilliant. As August and I were staring at what was left of the Colonel, he had lit two lanterns and handed me one. To keep these "creatures of the night" at bay, we used the lanterns. August, who was in the middle, shot ahead, splintering all in our path to create as much noise and distraction as possible.

Anything to keep them away!

We climbed as fast as we could, but our pace felt slow and it seemed as if these creatures were increasing in numbers. Two attacked my right ankle at the same time, and as I tried to shake them both off, one turned and bit into the other.

They chased us, never giving up, until we finally saw the light at the entrance to the cavern. We made a final push forward and fell out of the entrance onto a brilliant November sunlight.

We lay there for a moment, breathing hard – but only for a moment. I stumbled to my feet first, followed by August and Moss. Each of us, lost in our own thoughts, staggered back to our all-too familiar camp.

We collapsed again next to the remnants of last night's fire, gulping air and steadying our breathing. No one said a word for a few minutes. August eventually spoke first, her voice cutting the silence like a knife. "I don't want to spend tonight on top of this goddamn mountain! I want to go home!"

Moss looked at me and I at him. We both nodded in agreement. It was not long before we were heading back down the way we came up, with one less person amongst our crew. The horses were there as we arrived around dusk. We quickly hitched up the wagon and proceeded on our trek home.

Moss took the lead as we arrived at the main road to Beckleyville, while August drove the wagon. As we rode away, I turned back and gave the mountain one last look.

There, in the far-off distance, perched on the outermost ledge on top of the Five Finger Mountain, stood the creature.

I yelled at August and Moss, pointing to where the creature stood high above us, but when they looked up, the creature had all but disappeared in the fog.

CHAPTER 43
The Aftermath

I will never forget what I witnessed on that cold November night. I still dream of it today.

Not much was said in the aftermath, during our travel back to Cucumber and in the days and weeks after. However, after some time had passed, we began to speak of it, processing what had happened as best we could. Having heard my story, Moss and August had agreed with me that Black Damp should die. I had so much pain in my heart that I needed a reckoning. What we did – we felt – was an act of God.

But for those with vengeance... aren't they all?

It was August who thought of the cavern (and its occupants) as a way to inflict my revenge. I don't believe that August regretted her decision to stop me from obtaining her father's journal. I think her love for me, her need to ensure my safety, kept her from suffering any regret.

But I, dear reader... I suffer that shame. I still feel like I could have snatched the journal from under the demon's nose and possibly save the weeping souls it had taken.

Several years after our final trip down the cavern, Moss went on to become an ordained Baptist minister and founded the First Baptist Freedom Church, located in the new town of Beckley. His flock grew so large that both August and I helped construct an addition to his church in 1880. His legacy still lives on today in the hundreds of people he helped find God's word and the lives of salvation they led due to his calm, respectful, and peaceful presence.

Oh… and Jupiter Moss married.

Moss's wife was a stunning Chinese woman and daughter of a Buddhist monk. Her name was Nekhii Quan Nyx. But we just called her Nyx. As luck would have it, her father, mother and Nyx arrived in the United States just as the "War Between the States" ended. By this time, farms and plantations in the south were screaming for cheap labor and, upon seeing an advertisement Nyx, her father, and mother immigrated to South Carolina and there farmed corn, beets, and cotton on a plantation called Cherry Grove.

But one year later, a tremendous hurricane ravished the South Carolina coast, killing her parents and 32 other migrant workers. She said its wrath was so fierce that it drove the empty corn stalks right through the main house's wood lap walls.

There was, she said, nothing left of her parents to bury.

Homeless and with no money or family, Nyx decided to travel back to California and eventually catch a steamer back to her homeland in China.

She never made it.

It was a warm Sunday morning that Moss went to church early to prepare for the day's sermon when he encountered

Nyx sleeping on the front steps. He took her inside into the small rear office of the church and opened up a small cot. Once he convinced her that she was safe, he gently shut the door and let her sleep until church was over. There he took her to our home, and it was there we fed and offered her a place to get cleaned up and rest.

She remained with us for years to come, and the love that developed between she and Moss was both strong and tender, born out of a shared understanding of loss and perseverance.

Nyx's father was a Shaolin Monk, a warrior monk who was exceptionally skilled in the art of *Yijin Jing*.

And he taught everything to Nyx.

∞

Several years later after our final trip to The Five Finger Mountains, Moss and I sat together on the front porch on a warm southern night. I was holding a newspaper but not really reading it when Moss looked over at me with a solemn look upon his face. He sipped a sweet tea, swirling the ice around in his glass as he leaned against the porch rail, studying my face in the glow of the sunset on the horizon. He spoke softly but firmly, saying that he felt a calling from the Lord to "speak to me directly."

As long as we had known one another, we had never had such a talk. He sat down in his favorite chair next to me before speaking again. "You need savin."

"Me?" I replied defensively, running by fingers through my hair before looking down. "I adhere to the good book and I keep to most of God's commandments!"

"True," he said, "but you haven't been a practicing Christian since your Pa passed away. Your soul is just beggin to be saved. Nyx says that just as a candle cannot burn without a fire, a man cannot live without a spiritual life."

"She said that?" I replied, with some skepticism. It surprised me that Nyx cared anything about my spiritual life.

"Yes sir, she surely did," he replied in earnest. He smiled a quiet, warm smile as he patted my shoulder. I felt a warmth from him, and for a moment, I almost believed him. That I could be saved, my soul renewed, sins forgiven and washed away like summer heat in a cool rainstorm.

So, the following week after church and wearing my finest clothes, I stood along the banks of the New River (the same "River of Death") and I was baptized. August was there, with several of our friends and other church members. Afterwards, we had a huge picnic, celebrating my salvation.

And one year later, August and I were finally properly married (satisfying many of the old hens in town). Moss both gave her away and performed the wedding ceremony at the same time. We were married in the same barn where the All-Hallows E'en dance was held years before, and where my father died. Our love grew out of the ashes of tragedy, a phoenix rising to fly again.

At least, that's what we told ourselves.

August and I made a life for ourselves despite the demons that crouched in the corner of our minds, always watching and waiting to pounce. We had troubles, no doubt – dark days and nights where I felt as if I couldn't climb out of the hole – that cavern – that held all of my fears and furies. But we survived – and that's a hell of a lot more than most can boast.

Two years after my baptism, we had our only child, a daughter that we named Haven. August chose the name because the minute she met me, and saw our house for the first time, she knew that I and this home were going to be her sanctuary. A haven.

And our baby daughter made that complete.

CHAPTER 44

Haven

From an early age, it was evident that Haven was special –
and not only because she was *my* daughter. It was apparent
to all that met her that she was… *different*. She was highly
intelligent, and by the age of two, she was speaking in full
sentences, reciting her numbers up to 50, and beginning to
read. By the time she was five, she already could read the
classics. Her favorite was the Shaolin fighting manual *Yijin
Jing*, translated by Nyx.

Haven was extremely close to Moss and Nyx. The three
were inseparable. Often, late into the night after a rousing
game of Mumblety-Peg, I would find them on the porch,
Haven sitting crisscrossed on the floor or sprawled across
the porch swing, listening as Moss recited scriptures or Nyx
instructing her in the cultural study of *kung fu* and *Okinawan
Shorin-ryu* or *karate*. "Remember Haven-san, you must follow
the first precept of the *Yijin Jing*. One must abstain from any

type of killing. By non-hatred alone is hatred appeased. This is the first law eternal."

Afterwards, as August and I would put Haven to bed, we would walk out of the room and stop in the hallway, listening to her innocent, soft-spoken prayers.

Bullshit, I thought sometimes to myself as I listened to Moss or Nyx preach peacefulness and forgiveness. *Some sins aren't meant to be forgiven.*

However, despite this, we did try our best to raise her void of any hatefulness. After all, she was our daughter. Our one and only child.

At the age of six, August, Moss, Nyx and I decided that it was time to teach her more than what an average school aged child typically learns. Because of our past, we taught her what she needed to know to not be a victim. To be a she-wolf, like her mother – a survivor. We taught her how to shoot. Hunt. Moss and I showed her how to track in the woods.

And Haven was like a sponge – she absorbed it all.

When Moss or Nyx weren't siting with her, August and I were. We told her about both of her grandfathers and how we met. We left out the true nature of my father's death, the cavern, and the beast and horrors found below.

That was for another time.

She was very inquisitive – especially when it came to Boone and Caleb. She wanted to know everything about them. What they looked like, and how old they were, anything for her to weave a tapestry in her mind of her parents and the life they led before her. By the time she was 15, Haven was one of ten women who was accepted in the first class at West

Virginia University. It was not much longer after that she went away to school.

We did not see her again until Moss's death.

Several months before he died, Moss took a job with the local CSX Corporations rail line which was constructing a tunnel located next to the Greenbrier River. They called it the Big Bend Tunnel, due to the river running around Big Bend Mountain. Construction crews discovered early on that the mountain's hard shale resisted drilling and blasting, so they hired laborers to dig the tunnel by axe and pick.

Late on a Tuesday afternoon, we received word that Jupiter Moss, my friend and companion, was killed by a large rock slide in the tunnel. To say we were shattered would not be strong enough of a word to describe the grief that we felt.

And Haven was devastated.

A few days after we brought Moss's body home, I stood by his grave as the sun dipped below the mountains, fireflies just beginning to flash in the twilight glow. August and I buried Moss at our home, on the other side of my father's grave and by the first set of headstones we had made for Boone, Caleb, and the Major. I stood there, staring at the freshly packed dirt when I felt Haven's fingers gently slide into my hand. I turned and there she stood, looking exactly like her mother, tears streaming down her face. I just stared at her for a moment, numb to my own feelings in shock, until I broke down and held her in my arms. August stood on the porch, a shawl draped across her shoulders, watching, as we stayed that way for a long time until night's darkness forced us back inside.

Haven stayed in Cucumber until her mother – the love of my life – died a mere six months later. That is still too painful for me to write about. That also, hopefully, will also be for another time.

I believe that the pain of losing both her mother and Moss were just too much for Haven to bear, and after that, she packed up and left our home for good.

With both Moss and Haven gone, Nyx left several weeks later. I did not blame her. With only a few small possessions in a satchel, she bid me farewell. Before she left, she bowed deeply and said, "The way, Reecy-san, is not in the sky...but in your heart. Just as a snake sheds its skin, you must shed your past. Only then, Reecy-san, can you obtain the peace within your soul in which you so desperately seek."

CHAPTER 45
The Challenge

When my daughter left home, it was on a bright and cloudless Sunday morning. It was the day after we buried August. The night before, sitting around the fireplace after dinner, we began to talk and then argue, lasting well after midnight. It was now time to tell her the truth about everything.

I left nothing out.

I explained about Sarah and about Black Damp McCabe, about the cavern and the beast below. I told her about Moss and his history, what he had told me years ago about his life as a slave, and subsequently about his, and our...retribution.

Needless to say, Haven was dumbfounded. Afterwards, she sat in the glow of the fireplace, not saying anything for a long time, staring at the flames as they began to flicker and die. In the dim room, she looked so much like August that it nearly took my breath away.

"Dad... really?" she whispered softly, turning her gaze to look into my eyes. "This couldn't have happened. I don't believe you! This… could NEVER have happened!" Her voice grew louder as she stood up and began pacing the room.

I couldn't tell if she truly didn't believe me, or if she just refused to.

"I would never have done that. I don't believe in that. Do you understand? You murdered him!" she said, shaking her head. "Father… to have harbored such hate for Black Damp has poisoned your soul!"

I offered no apology.

Haven kneeled down to stoke the fire before turning back to face me again. She stood, walked over and took my hand. She made me promise to never go back to The Five Finger Mountains.

"Never, Dad… NEVER. Promise me!"

I looked at her emerald eyes, pleading. For part of my family was still there.

Haven jerked her hand back and stood, looking down at me. She was furious. "You're a stubborn old man! A fool of a Ragland who always lived in the past! Hatred is never appeased by hatred in this world!"

I said nothing, just looked away, and stared at the fire until Haven stomped away, up the stairs to bed. I stayed that way until the last of the flames finally went out.

ॐ

I was sitting on the porch early the next morning when Haven opened the old screen door with her two suitcases in hand and told me she had to go.

It was Christmas day.

I've had a lot of time to reflect since that morning, and I know that if it was me, I probably would have done the same thing.

There was no animosity. After all, she was my one and only child. She was now able to now take care of herself.

I – we – had taught her well.

She told me coolly that she had several "prior obligations" and that she would come back soon. I stood to hug her, and she held me tightly for a moment.

"Don't do anything, Dad," she said into my ear before letting me go.

I think she needed time to think. Think about her life, the loss of her mother and Moss, of the stories I had told her. I knew she thought that I was crazy – an unstable old man who was losing reality.

She took the wagon into Beckley and left on the evening train north. Tears rolled down my cheeks as I watched her ride away, but I wiped them away on the back of my sleeve. I took in a ragged breath before I stepped back inside our home, alone.

I knew then that I would never see her again.

People and moments we lose in life have a way of coming back in the end. But not always the way we expect.

That night I went to bed early. When I woke up the next morning, I left my bedroom and walked down the stairs to get a cup of coffee. The upper level of the home always seemed to be warmer than the first floor, so I was also going to put several logs in the fireplace when I stopped dead in my tracks, right in the middle of my stairs.

There, on the hardwood floor, right in the middle of the foyer lay the red ribbon of First Lieutenant Henr' Dumont. With parts of his blond ponytail still attached.

Beside the clothing, written in blood on the foyer floor, was a challenge:

COME...PLAY WITH ME

Right in my home.

It had been here, sometime in the night. The goddamn thing had been in my home while I slept!

It had waited and watched me all these years, choosing the perfect time and place to issue its dare. It had been patient, knowing that I would be alone, finally. And now it was ready.

It had issued a challenge, a duel.

The anger and hatred flooded my system, so intense that I could barely see.

I immediately accepted.

ᴏᴠᴏ

When spring arrived, I tore down the old barn adjacent to the house and used the pieces to construct a cabin. Well, more or less, a small hut... on top of the middle finger of that godforsaken mountain.

A month after Haven left, I walked out of the courthouse owning one thousand acres of the rawest, shit-piece of land this side of the Mississippi. I paid the exorbitant price of one cent per acre. I thought at the time the whole thing wasn't worth a plug nickel. So now the mountains, the hound from hell, and the hole... was all mine.

It took me every weekend and three days out of the week, but I managed to build the small, one-room cabin with a front entry porch and a stone fireplace for when the night air gets cold.

And it gets very cold in the early month of November. That, I know from experience.

The furnishings are sparse. I have a mattress on one side of the wall and an old desk I took from the house on the other side. I designed the cabin so that the front porch faces the forest, where the hole beyond will appear. The back porch has an absolutely brilliant view of the valley below.

Not all of my time has been spent on the cabin. At the bottom of the mountain, I erected a wood entry gate, and along that portion a barbed wire fence. From this side, the side closest to the main road, no one can go in or out except through the gate.

The gate I keep under lock and key.

Beside the cabin in the small clearing, I set various kinds of traps, snares, and set-ups. I constructed hook snares from several bent pine saplings. If the demon sets it off, a large metal hook will swing upwards, setting the barbs of the hook deep inside its flesh.

I dug several holes and camouflaged bear traps. I have not forgotten that this creature used the tops of the trees to navigate, so I set several large traps on the larger branches of the surrounding trees.

For some reason I wanted its death to be at the same time it took the others. Therefore, all was completed by late September. I stocked my hut with enough provisions to last until the end of the year. I bequeathed my horse to a local family in Cucumber, and with the same pack that I used during the war, began my last trek east toward the mountain.

I'm not sad, not really. I know that either way the end result would be for me to at least be reunited with my father, Boone, Caleb, Moss…and August. My dearest August.

They will be waiting for me, much like I had waited for them all through these years.

I left a letter in the house for Haven. I told her that I had gone, one last time, up to the mountains – to the very top, where it had all begun. I told her that I loved her so very, very much. And that Moss, August, and I were so proud of her, and that she that she truly was the embodiment of us all.

And I also left her the key to the gate.

CHAPTER 46
My End

It is now time, midnight on the awakening hour. As I write to you, I am now an old man.

My tale to you is one of warning. A warning so severe, so staggering that my end is simply the beginning.

I now sit on my porch at the top of the world, listening in the darkness, knowing that they are here. The creatures that chased me years ago are with me now… here in the woods.

I still have so much more to tell, so much to explain.

But time is not on my side.

As they dart around in the darkness, I know that they are waiting for him. The shadow creature, the demon from hell – the beast in the night.

They always wait for him.

I started this story decades ago, and I tried my best to keep a true account. Please believe me when I say these are not just the foolish ramblings of an old man.

I'm afraid. I've always been afraid. Since my first encounter, I have always looked behind my back. My hand shakes badly as I write down these last words. I can hardly put them on paper.

But know this, this tale isn't for one person but a warning... to us all. My journey is now complete, and now, it's up to you to remember.

If you have read my words, then you understand what's at stake. Heed my warnings and tread cautiously. You must be noble and unafraid. Brave enough to show both courage and compassion.

For under a pale moonlight, in the dead of night, it always approaches from below. You can try to run, you can try to hide, but you will never be able to mask what's inside.

For this is our journey. What we all must walk, what our future holds.

But there will come a night, under a dim firelight, with a distant howl of fright... that they will be coming home.

Signed on This Day of Our Lord
November 12, 1914

Reece Ragland

1968...South Vietnam

CHAPTER 47

Epilogue

It was pitch black at one in the morning when Captain Ned "Buzzy" Ragland landed at the Tan Son Nhut Air Base in Saigon, South Vietnam.

South fucking Vietnam, he thought as they touched ground on the small airstrip.

The base was the home of the L-19 Bird Dog and the T-28 Trojan counter insurgency, small aircraft used to shuttle both incoming and outgoing grunts in and out. From the stink. "The shit," he called it. It also served as the main base for the 293rd Helicopter Squadron. It was here that Buzzy was immediately taken. Ten minutes later and a quick trip to the latrine, and Buzzy was airborne once again.

His orders were to travel by chopper to a very little-known fire base near Cao Lanh, on the border of Laos and Vietnam. Near the Mekong Delta. "The Big Muddy." As he climbed aboard the UH-1 Huey, the side gunner extended a helping hand aboard. Smiling from ear to ear, the gunner introduced himself as Viper.

"Welcome aboard, Captain. First time in country?" he asked, looking him over.

"Why, ah… yes, it is. How did you know?" Buzzy replied, raising an eyebrow.

Viper started laughing and turned to the pilot, who was going through his pre-flight check list. "Told you. I can spot a cherry a mile away. Pay up, my man." He stuck his hand out towards the pilot.

First-timers were called "cherries"; this much Buzzy knew. He didn't say anything, though, and just sat down to buckle himself in.

"Jesus Christ," the pilot muttered, shaking his head. He reached into his pocket and pulled out a dollar and slapped the bill into Viper's hand.

"This here's Snake," Viper said, pointing to the pilot. Buzzy replied with a "nice to meet you,"but Snake had moved back to working on the pre-flight check list. He responded with a grunt. Minutes later, the gunship took off, staying low over the forest and heading southwest.

My god, this is great, Buzzy thought as they arched over some low-lying trees.

As they gained some altitude, the air became much cooler, much like the mountainous air he was so used to back home in West Virginia. It felt good. Better than the oppressing heat at ground level.

Buzzy looked up and could see a full sky of stars. *What an adventure,* he thought. At that moment, he felt at peace, and a deep gratitude that he volunteered for his country.

God and Country.

He looked over at Snake, who was chewing gum. "How far out are we?"

"What?" yelled Snake. "Can't hear you!" He pointed upwards toward the engine.

Buzzy waved his hand. "Never mind."

"What?" replied Snake again, this time looking a little annoyed.

Buzzy just shook his head and looked away. He glanced over to Viper and saw him smiling.

They were right – what a cherry.

Buzzy closed his eyes and allowed his thoughts to drift off to home, his girl, and to what may lay ahead. The people that he left back home. His parents and friends at West Virginia University, the college he attended before enlisting, told him he was crazy. But he felt that he needed to do this.

After all, God and Country.

He opened his eyes and could vaguely make out distant mountain peaks and lower valleys. He had no idea where he was.

Buzzy glanced down at his watch and it read four in the morning. He checked his gear and made sure his M-16 was fully loaded with the safety on. *God, what if he were killed the first day in country all because I forgot to load my rifle,* he thought wryly, trying to push down some the nerves in his belly.

He chuckled a little at that – first day in the country. He's survived four hours so far.

Pretty good.

Buzzy made sure his seatbelt was secure before leaning over toward the large side opening of the helicopter. Viper sat on a pad with half his body outside of the craft, one foot placed upon the wheel strut.

They gently banked to the right and for the first time, Buzzy saw a second gunship trailing them. For a brief moment, he caught sight of the white teeth encapsulating the front part of the craft, painted to look like a set of shark teeth.

It was meant to scare the hell out of the enemy.

As Buzzy watched the helicopter slice through the night, he could see why. It scared the hell out of him.

He looked away, focusing his gaze ahead. It was pitch black below. If the craft was to be shot down, he felt sure that the enveloping darkness would kill them first before any crash into the jungle.

Buzzy moved back inside, and leaned back against his seat. He again closed his eyes, and after a few minutes, he must have drifted off to sleep because suddenly he felt Viper kick his leg. "One hour!"

Buzzy gathered his gear. He turned toward the second chopper and saw the silhouette of the aircraft against the far-off pink glow of the sun, which was finally beginning to rise.

And that's when he heard it. It sounded like a small stone hitting the helicopter. A minute later, radio chatter burst through Snake's headset loud enough for all three of them to hear.

"Mike One… Mike One… Delta Charlie… gooks in the field… say again… gooks in the field."

"Say again, Delta Charlie... say again?" Snake said sharply into the headset, turning off the panel lights of the chopper.

"Stay low and green... I repeat, stay low and green. Six feet for the package... say again, six feet for the package."

Buzzy heard it again – another small "ping" hitting the helicopter. He tilted his head to peer outside when Viper grabbed his collar and motioned for him to take off his helmet.

"Captain! You need to take off your helmet! You need to take off your helmet and sit on it. We don't want you to get shot in the ass, do we sir?" Viper yelled over the sounds of the blades above.

"What... what... were those shells... gun shells... bullets hitting us?" Buzzy stammered, looking back and forth at Viper and Snake.

"Naw... sir," Viper replied, laughing. "Birds. I think those were really small birds."

The sun began to shine on the distant mountains, and Buzzy was finally able to see below. He saw no valley. No village. Nothing. Just lush jungle and tropical vegetation.

By now, Snake's headset was going wild. He heard people pleading and begging for pickup, for someone to answer.

"Mike One, mike one, mike one... do you copy? Over."

Snake replied that he was about ten klicks on the west side of the Muddy, coming in "hot and heavy."

As they crested over a large mountain, Buzzy finally saw a break in the jungle and spotted a sprawling valley just over the mountain's peak. He stared below for a moment before blinking and refocusing his gaze. He couldn't believe his eyes.

The whole valley was moving. The whole goddamn valley was moving! Moving with what seemed like the entire North Vietnamese Army in the direction of the small fire base which lay directly ahead.

His fire base.

As they began to make their approach, Buzzy could see hundreds, no thousands, of NVA Regulars moving towards the outpost. As they flew closer, Buzzy saw that many were shooting upwards in his direction.

Oh, shit, shit, shit, he thought. *My god, what have I gotten into?*

Approximately two klicks away, Viper started opening up, using a side M60 "slick" machine gun and firing indiscriminately below.

Buzzy grabbed his weapon to help return fire when he felt the helicopter shake from one side to the other. Looking out the side door, he saw and then heard two explosions ahead on the valley floor. Snake must have fired his two ARA's (Aerial Rocket Artillery) into the crowd below.

Viper yelled, motioning to Buzzy. "Sir, get your gear and be ready to jump! We'll be over for about two seconds, and you jump out!"

Buzzy felt his heart drop. "What? Woah – just wait a minute! I can't go down there!" he yelled back, trying to keep his panic from showing on his face.

"You'll be fine. Two minutes!" he replied, holding up two fingers.

The date was January 30, 1968. Buzzy didn't know then that the day would go down as one of the bloodiest in the

Vietnam War – the day of the Tet. It was the day the entire North Vietnamese Army launched devastating attacks all up and down South Vietnam. Cao Lanh would be the location of the worst attacks perpetrated against American Forces in the history of the United States.

Ever.

Buzzy's first day in the country.
Welcome to South Fuckin' Vietnam.

CHAPTER 48
Fire Base Goliath

Buzzy was panicking – big time. He had the advantage of being in a helicopter, to know what was coming.

And it was death.

The fire base seemed to be just a small round dot of dirt in an ocean of moving jungle. At this point, their gunship was taking heavy fire. It swooped in over the rear of the base towards a small, cleared circle marked with a large red *H*. He noticed a small road leading to the opposite side, and it seemed that most of the NVA were concentrating upon that area.

As the gunship lowered to about six feet above the ground, Buzzy looked over at Viper.

"Good luck, Captain," said Viper with a grim smile. He knew that most cherries don't last long. Not in Vietnam.

Buzzy grabbed his gear in his left hand and his M-16 in his right hand, and jumped.

As he hit the ground, he rolled over to prevent a harsh impact, but as he did so, he accidently let go of his gear.

But he still held on to his rifle tightly, like a mother holding her child. This was his lifeline, his security – what he knew he needed to survive.

Buzzy stood up and looked up to wave to the helicopter, signaling that he was okay, but the gunship was already well gone, slicing through the air as it sped away from the chaos below.

"You! Cherry! Get over here… NOW!" yelled a gunny sergeant nearby, standing under a tent fortified by sand bags halfway up along the sides.

As Buzzy reached to retrieve his gear, mortar rounds starting exploding in the camp. He stood up and began to make his way towards the sergeant.

The sergeant took a closer look at Buzzy. "Oh… ah, sorry about that, sir," he yelled at Buzzy approached, somewhat ruefully. "Didn't see the rank."

A mortar round exploded nearby and Buzzy flung himself into the bunker.

The sergeant didn't even flinch. "Welcome to Firebase Goliath, sir," he yelled, grinning over the explosions. "We don't normally get visitors around here."

Buzzy stood up and the two shook hands. "Sergeant… do you know what's coming? Buzzy said loudly. "The shit's going to hit the fan in about two minutes!"

The sergeant opened his mouth to speak, but suddenly, rifle fire opened up along the front of the base.

"Sir, you need to speak with Colonel Jameson on what you saw coming in. Come with me!" he yelled over the mortar and gunfire. As the sergeant turned, Buzzy heard a loud gunshot and watched in horror as his head simply *disappeared* in a mess of red goo and brain matter. He grabbed the sergeant's collar to hold him up, but it was too late. The sergeant's body – what was left of it – slumped to the ground, taking Buzzy with it. As Buzzy quickly stood up, he looked over the sandbags and saw the front line of Firebase Goliath had collapsed, and NVA was inside the perimeter.

In about 10 minutes, Firebase Goliath would be wiped off the face of the earth.

Buzzy grabbed his weapon and started toward the back of the camp. At this point, soldiers from both armies were involved in brutal hand-to-hand combat. As he weaved in and out, a Vietnamese soldier ran up to him and tried to stick him with a bayonet, but Buzzy's instinct took over. He parried to his left and raised his weapon and fired, killing the man instantly.

He moved on. Barely a minute later, he collided with another NVA soldier. She brought up her weapon to shoot, but Buzzy quickly slapped it away before raising his weapon and shooting her in the stomach. She let out a pained groan and immediately fell to the ground.

Buzzy didn't stop. He just kept running, weaving in and out. As he approached the south barricade of barbwire fencing and sandbags, he heard someone calling for him.

"Hey, you! You! Over here!" yelled an American soldier, who was outside of the perimeter firing into the firebase.

As Buzzy leapt over the barbwire, he heard the thuds of bullets hitting the sandbags. He turned around to face the man and he immediately recognized him as a Green Beret. Special Forces. Baddest of the bad asses.

The man looked Buzzy up and down quickly before turning his gaze back towards the carnage inside. "Name's Richards... Pete Richards," the soldier said as he indiscriminately fired back into the base.

"Ragland, er... Buzzy... Buzzy Ragland," Buzzy replied, trying to sound calm and collected, despite what he had seen and done in the past five minutes.

"We were fucked from day one!" replied Pete as he continued his fire. "We warned the Colonel time and time again, but he wouldn't listen. Some West Point guy."

He stopped firing and turned to look at Buzzy. "You ain't from West Point, are ya?"

"No... I'm not. I'm from Virginia... er, I mean, West Virginia." Buzzy replied. He picked up his rifle and began to also shoot back inside the camp.

As it is with most battles, to the victor come the spoils. Within several minutes it was obvious to both men that the battle, this battle, was over. Those left in Firebase Goliath didn't have a chance. Both men stopped shooting and hid behind the sandbags looking into the base.

What they witnessed that day was ghastly.

The North Viet Cong Regulars rounded up those soldiers who were alive and either shot them in the back of the head or stabbed them repeatedly with their bayonets until they were dead. Buzzy watched in horror though a small hole between sandbags as enemy soldiers looted the dead bodies. He watched as several of them took two American soldiers aside and decapitated both.

Crouched down below the sandbag, Pete loaded his M-16, muttering more to himself than Buzzy. "Sons of bitches. Those motherfuckers!"

Buzzy looked over at Pete and replied softly, "I'm sorry. You knew them well?"

"Naw, I just arrived three days ago from our camp located about 20 klicks south of here. On my way home from this hellhole. Naw, those sons of bitches took the beer," he said, pointing to two Viet Cong soldiers hauling provisions out of one of the nearby tents.

Pete glanced sideways at Buzzy with a sarcastic grin and winked. *I like this guy,* Buzzy thought to himself.

"Listen, we got to vamoose out of here," said Pete, who crouched down below the perimeter sandbags. "The trains arrived but I ain't gettin' on board, if ya get my drift."

Buzzy got his drift.

꧁

Firebase Goliath sat upon a small knoll, and because of this, it possessed a commanding view of the surrounding area. Pete and Buzzy took advantage of this and slowly slid down to the bottom, disappearing into the surrounding jungle.

"Our best bet is to hump it and go back to my old stomping grounds. We got a bunch of crazies that would be dying to offer some payback," Pete said, looking back up at Goliath.

"You said about 20 klicks. How long will that take?" Buzzy asked as he reloaded his rifle.

"About a day and a half, give or take. Depends on if we run into any more of them." Pete turned and looked over to Buzzy "You cool with that?"

Buzzy swallowed and focused on his rifle. "I'm cool," he replied. *It's not like I have any other choice,* he thought grimly.

So off they went, slicing their way through the thick jungle and trying not to think too much about what lay ahead. Buzzy tried to copy and learn everything he could from Pete, watching as he expertly carved a small path through the jungle with a machete. Pete led the way, with Buzzy following closely behind, rifle raised. Buzzy knew that they just need to stay the course and make good time.

But time was not on their side.

About an hour into the trek, they came across a small, worn-out path leading north to south. Pete stopped and motioned for Buzzy to kneel down.

"We stay off the path as much as possible, ok?" he whispered sharply. "Don't want to run into any gooks in the field."

Buzzy nodded in agreement. As he began to stand up, Pete motioned for him to kneel back down. Then suddenly he grabbed Buzzy and both of them fell back into the thick jungle foliage. Pete lay on top of Buzzy and motioned for Buzzy not to move.

"Don't move! Someone's coming!" he hissed.

Sure enough, about 15 seconds went by when a group of Viet Cong soldiers ran by them. Not one noticed that they were only feet away.

Pete lay on Buzzy for another minute to make sure that there were no stragglers on the trail. He then got up and offered his hand to Buzzy to help him to his feet.

"There probably won't be any more on the path for a good while, so let's stay on it, instead. We can make better time."

Their luck ran out about 15 minutes later when, as they rounded a sharp turn in the trail, Pete came face-to-face with a small boy of about 10 years old. The boy carried an old SMG STEN gun, probably carried over from the war with the French decades ago. The young boy raised his weapon as Pete raised his hand to stop him.

The boy shot Pete right through the chest.

Pete died before he hit the ground.

Buzzy, who was behind Pete, had raised his weapon but could not fire because Pete was in the way. As Pete's body fell lifeless to the ground, the boy's eyes locked in on Buzzy. The boy fired; however, the gun jammed. He looked at Buzzy with wide eyes as Buzzy aimed his rifle.

And that's when Captain Ned "Buzzy" Ragland woke up.

1974...Beckley, West Virginia

CHAPTER 49

The End is...just the Beginning

It was about five in the morning on a cool November Saturday when Buzzy Ragland woke up from the dream – the same dream he had experienced since his combat days. As he lay there drenched in sweat, he kept seeing Pete in his mind.

The man who saved his life... but who he could not save.

If not for Pete, Buzzy knew that he would not have made it that first day. After Pete's death, it took him four months of living off the jungle and avoiding Viet Cong patrols before he made it to the Special Forces base camp. With help from several gunships, they were able to retake Firebase Goliath.

Normally after the dream, Buzzy would get up and fix himself a cup of strong coffee and sit in his recliner, remembering. But this morning was going to be different.

Buzzy had plans for this morning. He was extremely anxious to explore the one thousand acres of vacant land left to him by his grandmother years before. He had been on the property several times previously, but had never spent an entire day there.

As he rose from bed, he ticked off a mental list of what he needed to bring with him that day. He had about an hour before sunrise, enough time to pack an extra set of clothes (in case it rained), his 45 handgun (always with him wherever he went), several bottles of beer, water, and a bag of trail mix. After making sure he had enough money to fill up his truck, he left a note for his wife, who was still sleeping, and threw his gear in the back of his truck.

Crap, he thought, *the gate key*. He went back into the house and walked into his den pulling open his desk drawer. He pulled out an old rusty key chain, hooked to one faded copper key and a very old pin knife. On the side of the pin knife was an inscription.

Old Timber.

If that knife could only have talked.

Buzzy put the chain with the key and knife into his pocket and quietly slipped out of the house again. As he pulled away from the house, he rolled down the windows, slipped in an old Hank Williams cassette, and turned up the volume.

"There's a tear in my beer cause I'm cryin' for yoooooo-ouuuuuuu."

Buzzy let the cool November breeze flow through the window and sat back, enjoying every minute of it.

As he drove, he thought of his Nana Haven. They always had a special relationship, more of a mother-son than grand-mother to grandson. She, more than anyone else in his life, had taught him about survival in the woods. She taught him things like what to eat and what not to eat, how to find the sweetest wild onions. She was particularly skilled in locating wild ginseng. How he wished she could be there with him today – he still felt like he had so many questions left unanswered. He shook his head, and smiled at a memory of her in the forest, stooped down low, picking wild thyme. At home in the forest, trees and lush greenery enveloping them both, blocking out sky and sun.

His thoughts then turned to Pete again.

Buzzy drove the old way, winding down Beckley Road. He wanted to just enjoy the day -his day in the woods. Tiring of ole' Hank, he reached into the console and, without looking, grabbed another cassette and popped it into the truck's player. It took several seconds for a song to pop up, and with the volume already turned up the words boomed out:

"Please allow me to introduce myself
I'm a man of wealth and taste
I've been around for a long, long year
Stole many a man's soul to waste."

Ugh, Buzzy thought, *must have been one of the kid's tapes.* He reached down and pulled out the cassette and decided to not listen to anything.

It took him about two hours to finally reach the Sam Black Church exit. After 13 more miles, he turned left onto a small dirt road. During Buzzy's first visit to the property, it became very apparent then that the ground was barren. Desolate. He noticed that it had not changed since his last visit.

No new growth, nothing.

Jesus, why would anyone want to buy this is beyond me, he thought to himself as he continued his drive.

Fifteen minutes later, he arrived at the bottom of The Five Finger Mountains. Buzzy knew he was at the entrance, because his grandmother had posted a sign which was in her recognizably, wonderful handwriting.

TRESSPASSERS WILL BE SHOT ON SIGHT!
AND THAT MEANS YOU!

He smiled. That was her to a T.

He grabbed his backpack – the same one he used in Vietnam – put on his side holster with his loaded 45, and locked the doors to the truck.

Unlocking the gate proved to be more challenging. The lock was very rusty, and after about ten minutes, it finally succumbed to his jimmying the key.

Buzzy left the gate unlocked – he didn't want to go through that hassle again. He then began to hike around two small mountains before going upwards, following a small dirt path. Every so often, he would stop and sit down on an old log or large stone, turning to marvel at the wondrous, panoramic view beginning to open up.

Now he understood. The view and isolation had to be the major selling point for this property. And the higher up he went, the more spectacular the view.

He neglected to notice that there were no animals, no birds, no insects… nothing was moving in the woods.

As he made his approach to the summit of the middle mountain, he broke into a small clearing where he was surprised to find a decrepit, single-room cabin.

"God, how did anyone get this lumber up here?" he muttered to himself. He walked around the cabins outside, and noticed both a front and back covered porch. As he entered into the cabin from the back, he saw that the left side portion of the roof had collapsed and that most of the wood flooring had rotted away.

Along the right side of the wall were remnants of an old bed, with a shredded, torn mattress. To the left side was a table, crumpled due to the weight of the roof and ceiling.

There was nothing else.

Buzzy exited the front part of the cabin, facing the top of the mountain. As he stepped out, he caught sight of a swatch of large scratch marks on the edging of the door. Carefully, he danced around rotted floor boards on the porch and saw that several of the wood slats were badly stained.

Buzzy knelt down and examined the discoloration. It looked like old blood.

He stood up and shrugged to no one. Hunters. The blood stains were likely that of a deer.

Carefully stepping off the porch, he proceeded upwards through a patch of barren trees toward the top of the mountain. The view would be breathtaking. It would, he thought, lead him closer to God.

As he stepped out of the tree line, however, what he immediately noticed was not the spectacular view (although it was).

But a huge, HUGE hole in the ground.

"JESUS!" he gasped, this time out loud. He stood rooted to the spot, his mind unable to process what he was seeing.

It was then, while he was staring in disbelief, that a small head, followed by a child's body, exited the right side of the chasm.

What the hell...? Buzzy thought as he stood there frozen, watching this small boy exit from this immense cavern in the ground. As the boy slowly climbed out, he immediately collapsed on the ground and lay there still. Buzzy shook his head, finally breaking free of his shock, and rushed over to the child.

The boy's breathing was labored, and his appearance was horrifying. His clothes appeared to be a patchwork of rags. The top of his shoes were missing, and all that was left was barely enough to fit each foot. Each sole was bound by tied together shoe strings and cloth. His hat (what was left of it) encompassed just the edging and a worn-out brim. There was no belt holding up his pants, just a section of ragged rope.

His body was pretty cut up, with a large tear in his flesh along his left leg, He cradled his right arm, a deep bite exposing strips of flesh and tendon. He lay there for a moment, catching his breath and muttering to himself as Buzzy tried to figure out what to do next. But before Buzzy could make a move, the boy startled him by rising to his feet, shakily but with what seemed like incredible willpower. He looked up and his eyes locked on Buzzy.

Buzzy had seen this look before. The "thousand-yard stare" of a man who had been through the shit... and survived.

With his right hand, Buzzy slowly reached down and unlocked his holster. He had also seen that look once before on the face of a small child, not too much younger than this one.

The boy did not seem to notice. For what seemed like several minutes, the two just stared at one another. Both in complete disbelief at what they were seeing.

Then the boy started to move towards Buzzy. Not knowing what to do, he just stood there as the boy stepped closer towards him.

He can't be more than 10, 12 at the most, Buzzy thought.

As the child approached, he reached out and took Buzzy's right hand, placing it into his and looking up.

Buzzy looked down and saw haunted, mournful eyes.

"Suh," the boy said looking up at him. "Suh… we g…g-ots to go… we gots to go… NOW!"

Buzzy didn't move. "Wha… what… what did you say?" Buzzy replied, staring down at the boy.

The boy started to gently pull Buzzy away from the hole.

"'Suh… we gots to go… N…N-OW!" said the boy, this time more urgently and with a panic in his voice.

"What? Who are you?" Buzzy asked.

"My name is Caleb. Don't really have a last name. And we don't have time for this neither. It's coming! Quickly we hafta go… NOW!"

"What… who's coming?" replied Buzzy as the boy clawed at him, yanking on his arm to pull him away from the hole.

"The Hunter."

www.ingramcontent.com/pod-product-compliance
Lightning Source LLC
Chambersburg PA
CBHW021947170626
46808CB00001B/56